Billie of Fish House Lane

Meredith Sue Willis

Also by Meredith Sue Willis

Fiction

A Space Apart
Higher Ground
Only Great Changes
Quilt Pieces
(with Jane Wilson Joyce)
In the Mountains of America
Trespassers
Oradell at Sea
Dwight's House and Other Stories
The City Built of Starships

Children's Fiction

The Secret Super Powers of Marco
Marco's Monster

Nonfiction on Writing

Personal Fiction Writing
Blazing Pencils
Deep Revision

Billie of Fish House Lane

Meredith Sue Willis

Montemayor Press

Millburn, New Jersey

Printed in the United States of America.
For information contact
Montemayor Press,
P. O. Box 526, Millburn, NJ 07041
Web site: MontemayorPress.com

1 3 5 7 9 10 8 6 4 2

Library of Congress Cataloging-in-Publication Data

Willis, Meredith Sue.
  Billie of Fish House Lane / by Meredith Sue Willis.
    p. cm.
  Summary: A twelve-year-old girl attempts to understand and
accept her affluent, white cousin while living in a multiracial,
eccentric family.
    ISBN 1-932727-02-7 (pbk. : alk. paper)
  [1. Racially mixed people--Fiction. 2. Family life--Fiction.
3. Cousins--Fiction.] I. Title.
    PZ7.W68317Bi 2005
    [Fic]--dc22   2004028399

To the children
of the Newark Public Schools

especially the good writers at

Bragaw Avenue School
Camden Street School
Maple Avenue School
Morton Street School

and

Ridge Street School

Billie of Fish House Lane

Meredith Sue Willis

Chapter One

Fish House Lane

We had the party for the girls' basketball team on the last day of school. We all wore our best shorts, and I had new summer sneakers. I'll be a starter on the team next year even though I'm not the best shooter. My specialty is keeping on the move. Whatever I do, in basketball or life, I keep on the move. This is one way I am the opposite of my best friend Eutreece Robinson. Eutreece doesn't play sports. She reads and thinks about mysteries and tells other people what to do. I like to tell people what to do, too, but I like to do it on the move.

At first, because of tests and the sixth graders' class trip and graduation, it looked like there would be no basketball party, but we told Coach we *had* to have a party, so we did. We had an ice cream cake with icing basketballs and hoops. We cheered each other and the coach. We hugged the sixth graders good-bye, and we talked about how we'll be even better next year. The sixth graders all promised to come back for all our games. Then we cried and hugged some more, and finally my little brother Trane and I left.

1

Trane was at the party because we have a rule in our family that no one walks out Fish House Lane alone. Our house is the last house in the City. It is so far out in the marshes that it's like you aren't in a city at all. Well, it's not like the country either, because you can see overpasses, electrical towers, old warehouses, and a canal. But we like living there, especially since it's our first house since my mother and dad got back together.

There are five in my family: me, Trane, Mom, Daddy, and Baby Parker. I don't count Mama Mae, because she has her own house and just visits us a lot. She's my Daddy's mother, and we lived with her the terrible year when my family broke up. Mostly it was Daddy and Mom who broke up, but it felt like it broke all of us. I was a lot younger then.

My Daddy was a famous artist before he got sick. He and my mom lived in New York City, and I was born in New York, but not Trane and not Parker. My Mom used to sing with a guitar in clubs, but now she sews African robes, even though she's like the opposite of African. Daddy's art was to carve up telephone poles and old logs. The legs of my bed are made out of his logs, each one with a different face. I named my four legs: the long dark face was Daddy; the big-eyed one was Trane; the round one was my mother; and the one that moves a little bit is Darling Billie. That's Daddy's nickname for me.

After Daddy got sick, Mom and Daddy put their priorities in order, and our family was reunited. Then we moved out here, and they celebrated by having Baby Parker. So you can see that things have gotten much, much better.

To get to our house by car, you have to drive around an abandoned factory building, but us kids have a short cut path that goes along the nasty oily canal through weeds that are higher than your head. We have to be careful when we go that way, because it's muddy, and also it goes near the house of a man named Neighbor who drinks alcohol and sets traps to catch rats. Neighbor's house is half on stilts in the canal, and he built it himself. He caught us spying on him once and made us sit on his porch while he made a speech about how we should never waste our time while we're young, and his son was almost a professional baseball player but lost his chance and now works downtown in a comic books and collectibles store. There was more, but it got very confusing. We were polite and listened to him talk, and he ended by giving us his old rowboat. We keep it hidden on the canal near my house for spying, and even though we're sort of friends with Neighbor now, we still spy on him when we feel like it.

Some people would probably say our house is even weirder than Neighbor's. Our house is painted two colors of blue: aqua and robin's egg. It sits at the very end of the road with marshes behind it and a highway bridge almost over top of it. But in spite of the bridge, it's private. We like the privacy, and also houses on Fish House Lane are very cheap.

Some people might also say my family with its two colors of parents is weird too. But they had better say Unique instead of Weird to my face. Even though I am an excellent student and a very polite young lady, I am also fierce, especially when I let my hair spread out behind me. Usually I tie my hair back or let Eutreece do it in Nubian braids, but when I'm fierce, it spreads out like wings on the wind. My hair is not an African sculpture like Eutreece's, and it isn't floppy, flat, and yellowish brown like my mother's. My hair is the exact same color of light brown as my eyes and my skin. My hair is almost

3

impossible to comb, but I always comb it anyway, because you have to respect yourself, especially when your family is unique.

There is one other house on Fish House Lane besides ours and Neighbor's. That's the Robinsons'. Another way we were lucky when we moved out here was because Fish House Lane had friends for everyone. Eutreece is my age, Martin is almost Trane's age, and there is even a tiny girl just a year older than Parker. They also have a grown sister who is a cosmetologist and a grown brother who is going to take the test to go to the police academy, plus Mr. and Mrs. Robinson and their really old relative that everyone calls Aunt Lucy.

Their house has a porch for each floor. Eutreece usually sits out on the top porch and reads. She wasn't there the day of the basketball party, but her father was out front cleaning a giant grill made out of a metal barrel. It was a surprise to see Mr. Robinson, because he usually sleeps in the day. All the grown up Robinsons except Aunt Lucy have jobs. Mr. Robinson has three different jobs, and Mrs. Robinson is a private duty nurse who lives with rich old people until they finish dying.

"Good afternoon, Mr. Robinson," Trane and I said.

"Hey, children," said Mr. Robinson. "I hope you got your appetites ready for the Robinson Family Fish Fry this Saturday. Ribs and barbeque and fried chicken!"

"Oh yes," I said. "We're looking forward to it."

Trane said, "Mr. Robinson, if it's a fish fry, aren't you supposed to have fish?"

I was embarrassed that he asked, but I'd been wondering too.

Mr. Robinson shows his gold side teeth when he laughs. "That's what folks used to call it Down South," he

4

said. "It's just a barbeque. You can cook what you want. We always did call it a fish fry."

"We're looking forward to it very much, Mr. Robinson," I said. "Is Eutreece in the house?"

"No, I think she went over your way." Then he added, "Listen, children, you bring all your friends you want to, and all your family to the Robinson Family Welcome-to-Summer Fish Fry, you hear? Everyone's invited. Be sure to bring your mother!"

The Robinsons try to be especially polite to my mother because she is White, and everyone else on Fish House Lane is Of Color. I am light tan, and Trane is mahogany, and Baby Parker is the color of caramel candy. Eutreece counts those as colors, but not white. I say, "Look here, Eutreece, if white wasn't a color, then you couldn't see my mother."

This is the kind of thing Eutreece and I can talk about for hours.

Actually, Eutreece likes my mother, maybe more than I do. My mother gets on my last nerve, especially when she cries for happiness or when she sings one of her sad folk ballad songs or when she stays in her nightgown all day while she sews African robes and she isn't African.

We were about halfway down the road to our house when we saw Martin Robinson. He jumped up and down. "Billie!" he yelled. "Billie! Billie! Eutreece said! Eutreece said Billie! Billie! Your Mom said!"

He stayed where he was, hopping up and down and yelling. "Calm down, Martin," I said. "You're popping like a toaster."

Trane started to laugh. "Martin's toast! Burnt toast!"

Martin's face was getting ready to cry or fight, so I said, "Now Martin, tell me again. Slowly."

5

"Eutreece says, Billie, get your butt to Surveillance Place! And your Mom says, Get in the house!"

"Everybody is telling me what to do," I said. "Martin, is my mother in the front of the house or the back?"

"She's inside feeding the baby," he said.

That meant she'd be sitting down away from the windows trying to get Parker to fall asleep after he nursed. So I said, "Trane, you take my backpack, and you and Martin go to our house, but go real slow. Take your time and tell Mom I'll be there in a minute. Okay?"

They are pretty good, Trane and Martin. They can be a real pain when they're playing around, but you can depend on them if they know you are serious. Martin stopped hopping, and Trane stopped teasing, and I slipped around the back way. My dog Panther was tied up there, and I stopped and petted her and told her she was a good dog, which isn't really true, behaviorwise, but I love her. Then I went past our vegetable garden into the swamp.

Eutreece and I built Surveillance Place ourselves. Eutreece said that if an old drunk crazy man like Neighbor could build an actual house by himself, then we could build a little lean-to. Trane and Martin carried stuff, but we built it. We use it to spy on the canal. It is in the shape of an A, like a tent made of two plywood sheets leaning together. There are more plywood sheets for the floor, and blankets for a door and walls. We have a nice plastic lounge chair where Eutreece sits and two partly broken chairs. The canal side has a window flap so you can spy on the deserted warehouse on the other side.

Eutreece was relaxing in the lounge chair with a bottle of cherry soda. She is the largest and smartest person I know of my age. She is as solid as if Daddy had carved her out of wood. Her eyes are a little slanted and her skin

6

is satiny, and she never runs. If she has to speed up, she just sort of glides. I don't tell Eutreece, but sometimes I wish my mother was like her instead of pale and wobbly and emotional. I know that sounds stupid for a kid my age to wish another kid the same age was her mother, but Eutreece is very mature, and she always knows exactly what she thinks.

The thing about me and Eutreece is that even though we're different, from the first time we met, we have been able to look each other in the eye and know things that most people have to talk about. Even when we are mad at each other, we understand exactly why.

I could see from Eutreece's eyes that something was going on. I sat down in the plastic chair with a bent leg, and she handed me the bottle of lotion that we rub on to keep the mosquitoes away. She had my Daddy's expensive black binoculars around her neck.

I said, "What are you doing with Daddy's binoculars?"

"I told your mother I needed them."

Knowing Eutreece, she probably just knocked on the door and said please lend me the binoculars. For me to get those binoculars, Mom would make me wait for Daddy to wake up and then I'd have to have a long i with him about the proper care of lenses.

I said, "Well, you better not put your thumbs on the lenses."

She gave me a look that is supposed to make you go shaky inside, but I don't. That's another reason we're friends, because I'm not afraid of Eutreece.

"What?" I said. "What?"

"Billie," she said. "Billie, Billie, Billie," like I was this totally stupid little baby girl. "Just look over across the canal at the warehouse and tell me what you see."

"Let me have the binoculars,"

7

It took me a while to get them adjusted. I could see weeds, reeds, mud, our leaky rowboat, canal water, more mud and gravel, then the wall of the abandoned warehouse. I could feel mosquitoes and other bugs bouncing on my arms in spite of the lotion, and way in the distance I could hear cars passing over the highway bridge and an airplane taking off. "Nothing," I said. "I see nothing."

Eutreece really knows how to be annoying. She slows herself down to one quarter speed and says each word like it's in a plastic box. "Oh. . . yes. . . you. . . do."

I looked again. I let the binoculars fall onto my chest. "I'm going in the house. My mom wants me."

"Neighbor buried something."

"Where?"

"Beside that pile of metal next to the warehouse."

I looked again. I could see the wall of the warehouse, and I could see the stack of rusty barrels and engine parts leaned up against the wall. "I still don't see anything."

"Then you don't see good." I gave her a look now, but my looks aren't nearly as strong as hers. I get restless and give up staring. "Beside the pile of metal, there's stirred up dirt." I looked again, and *maybe* just maybe I could see a ruffle in the dirt. She said, "I was just doing a little surveillance, and here came Neighbor in his good row boat. He pulled it up on that side, and he got out. He had a small shovel and a Bargain Bob shopping bag. He dug a hole and buried the thing in the bag. It's written in my Observations notebook." She keeps all these notebooks she calls Notes and Observations. "He looked from side to side, and then he buried the thing, and then he got back in his rowboat. And *we* have to find out what it is."

I didn't care very much—maybe because it was hot, and maybe because I was still thinking about basketball and being a sixth grader next year and the oldest in our whole school.

Eutreece said, "You don't bury something unless you don't want people to know what it is."

"Maybe he just wanted to put it in a safe place."

"Maybe," said Eutreece. "Either way, it's a mystery, and we're going to find out what's going on."

Sometimes I think she reads too many books. But just then we heard feet on the boards and Trane shouting "Billie! Billie! You have to come, Billie!" He came right in the blanket door, with Martin behind him. "Billie, Mom says you *have* to come right now!"

"We'll do what we talked about right after you see your mom," said Eutreece.

"What?" said Trane. "What are you going to do?"

"Surveillance," said Eutreece.

"None of your business," I said, and I led the parade through the reeds along the boards. You'd think after school is out, you'd get a rest from people giving you orders.

Chapter Two
The White Side

Mom was waiting for me on the beat-up old glider we keep on our porch. She was jiggling Parker, who was still awake, and her bare arms were jiggling too, like dishes of vanilla pudding sprinkled with nutmeg. "Billie!" she called. "Billie! Hurry up! I have something to tell you! I was just on the phone! I saw *him* downtown this morning and now *she* phoned!"

She was wearing one of her nightgown dresses, with little stripes and some lacy stuff. It wasn't really a nightgown, but it looked like one. When she goes to town, she dresses up in one of the African robes she sews for the boutiques.

"You're not going to believe it," she said. "I ran into my cousin Richie downtown! He was on was on his way to Court—"

"Who?" I said. My mom never, ever talks about her side of the family.

"The Boutique Afrique is right across from the Courthouse—" My mom sort of blinked in the sun like she had been seeing what she was talking about instead of what was in front of her. She said, "Why don't you children

10

come in and I'll give you something to drink and tell you all about it."

So we went in, and she gave me Parker, who was all hot and sticky and milky smelling. You could tell he wanted to go to sleep and also wanted to be part of the fun of sitting around the kitchen table and having Mom's Spicy Icy tea. Spicy Icy is red like Kool-Aid but has this good bitterness. It needs lots of honey. Mom also put out a plate of molasses and sunflower seed cookies, which look lumpy but taste delicious. That's how most of the food around our house is: it tastes better than it looks. When I was little, I didn't know our food was weird. I only found out how different we were the year we lived with Mama Mae, who used to be a school teacher. She taught us manners and regular dinner hours and a whole lot of things we don't use much except when she's around.

Once we were all around the table with Spicy Icy and cookies, my Mom clapped her hands. "Well!" she said. "This is quite a day. Let me tell you about Richie first. Richie was always my favorite cousin."

I glanced over at Trane, but he was whispering to Martin Robinson. Eutreece was concentrating on something on her plate, because while she really likes to eat, she is cautious about foods she doesn't recognize, which is most of the food at my house.

It was like nobody but me got it. Mom was talking about the White Side of the family. The White Side is all of Mom's relatives, and the only thing she ever used to say about them was that she divorced them long ago.

"Richie?" I said. "Who is Richie? I don't know any Richie."

"Richie is my mother's brother's son," said Mom.

She said this so normally, as if we had actually met these people! We didn't even know our grandmother on the white side! Supposedly I met her once, but all I remember is a pink coat and perfume.

"Well," said my Mom, "my cousin Richie—"

"Who I've never even heard of before," I reminded her.

"Listen to the story. I left my family early. I thought everything in the world was wrong with them, like all their values, and I just walked out and left them, the good with the bad."

"You're *estranged*," said Eutreece, showing off her vocabulary. Eutreece and I both got picked to take a special test to see if we get scholarships to a private school. We don't find out till later in the summer, and I said I wouldn't go anyhow because of my basketball team, but Eutreece said only a fool wouldn't go.

"Estranged," said Mom, with a big sigh, breaking a cookie into pieces. "That's exactly it. I walked out on my family and I became a stranger and they became strangers and we were deeply estranged."

I pretended nobody was there but me and Parker. I kissed his big head with the little clumps of soft hair like cinnamon clouds. He was getting heavy in my lap, which meant he was either falling asleep or filling up his diaper.

It turned out he was planning to grab a cookie. He missed, but I broke off a tiny piece for him.

Mom said, "No seeds, Billie."

I know very well that you have to be careful what babies eat. Sometimes I think I'm the only one around here's who's careful. I scraped off the seeds with my fingernail. I mean, Mom will even hand off Parker to Trane if she has something to do, and Trane is about as responsible as Panther.

12

"Yes," said my mom, telling her story to Eutreece, who is good at sitting and listening. For someone who says White isn't a color, Eutreece is always extremely interested in things like whether my mom sunburns and what does she do to make her hair so flat.

My mom said, "I've been estranged from my family all these years, except not from Richie. I always liked Richie, I just never see him. He and I used to have fun together. He was the kind of boy who wore a white dress-up shirt and an attaché case, even to school."

"Why?" said Trane. "Why did he wear a dress-up shirt to school?"

"Oh, I don't know. I think he was born wanting to be a lawyer. He used to wear a tie and sometimes a sports jacket too, and the other kids made fun of him, but Richie didn't care."

Eutreece was getting interested, because one of her dreams, along with detective and F.B.I. agent, is to be a lawyer. "And he did it? Become a lawyer when he grew up?"

"Oh yes," said Mom. "That's why I ran into him near the Courthouse. He's a very big lawyer, just like he planned. Fancy suit, fancy briefcase, cell phone, fancy car. He doesn't look funny anymore, though."

"What kind of car?" asked Eutreece.

Now Eutreece was asking personal questions about people who were related to me and not her. I know her parents tell her not to ask questions, but my mother didn't seem to notice Eutreece was being impolite.

"I didn't see his car," said Mom. "We were on the street and I suppose his car was in a parking lot. But we hugged and started talking like we were still kids in the back yard."

13

Parker dropped the piece of cookie, and his head drooped over to one side. He was going to sleep after all.

Mom said, "And it turns out that Richie and his family live less than an hour from here. Isn't that the most bizarre thing? I knew he had a son, but he has a daughter too, and get this, Billie, she is just the same age as you. Her name is Celia."

Now that was interesting. I adjusted Parker's weight in my arms. I had a girl cousin on the white side of the family.

"What about me?" said Trane. "Isn't that my cousin too?"

"Second cousins," said Mom. "She's a second cousin to both of you. And she sounds like a very talented, interesting girl. Richie and I said we just had to get you children together. And this morning, as soon as I got back, the phone rang, and it was Richie's wife Barbara! He called her from work, and they want Billie have a sleepover and get to know Celia."

"What about me?" said Trane. "I'm a second cousin too!"

I said, "Well, I hope you didn't say I would go, because I'm not going."

"I said I'd ask you," said Mom. "You know I would never make plans without asking you first."

I suppose that's one of the good things about my family. We're supposed to make our own decisions about things. I said, "I don't want to go to a sleepover with some rich girl I never met."

"They aren't *rich*," said Mom. "I mean, I'm sure they're affluent. They have a swimming pool— "

That shut us all up. We kids all looked at each other. I said, "You mean like a *private* swimming pool?"

"Yes."

"In-ground?"

"I don't know, I suppose."

Trane started to howl. "You mean they got a in-ground swimming pool and Billie gets to go and I don't?"

I said, "I'm not going."

"Let me go!" said Trane.

"Let me go!" said Martin Robinson.

I said, "I don't know why these people think we're going to go running to them just because they invite us. How come you never told me about them? How come you didn't tell me I had a second cousin girl on your side?"

"I didn't know about her," said my mom. "I knew about the older brother, but not about her. We lost touch." She said, "Richie has to fly to the coast this week, and Barbara thought it would be a good opportunity for Billie to come over. If you want to."

Eutreece was scrunching down her eyebrows like this wasn't going the way she wanted. She said, "I was supposed to invite you all to Fish Fry week-end. Billie, you're coming to Fish Fry, aren't you?"

"Yes, I'm coming to Fish Fry," I said.

And Mom said she was coming too, and she said she was going to make some whole wheat bread and rolls.

I said, "About that cousin."

"Celia," said Mom.

"Celia. I doubt I'll want to go, but I'll think about it."

Eutreece didn't like it. She didn't like me having a no-color cousin with an in-ground swimming pool, but she especially didn't like the idea of me going there for a sleepover.

Mom noticed that Parker had fallen asleep on me. "I'll put him down for his nap," she said, and came and got him off my lap.

15

As soon as she was out of the room, Eutreece said, "You can go visit your swimming pool cousin some other time. We have something to do."

"The Fish Fry?"

She rolled her eyes. "No! Surveillance!" She wanted me to help her dig in the dirt next to the warehouse. For somebody so mature, sometimes Eutreece seems very childish.

I said, "I'll make my decision later."

Trane did a lah-de-dah lady voice: "I'll make my decision later!"

I threw Parker's chewed cookie at him, and right away, he started throwing cookie pieces back at me, and lucky for him they never made it across the table.

"Clean it up," I told Trane. "Clean up every crumb and use a wet cloth too. Let's go, Eutreece."

Trane said, "You're going to go spying. We're going too!"

"You aren't going anywhere until this kitchen is clean."

Eutreece told Martin to help clean up, too, and then their friend Hector Hernandez showed up, and we made him stay and clean up too. Eutreece and I headed out the door and back toward Surveillance Place. It was a drippy hot day, and I was thinking about what it would be like to sink into my rich cousin's pool.

Chapter Three
The Warehouse

When Panther saw us, she went crazy and tried to break her rope, but I said, "Down!" in a firm voice, and we cut through the garden. Mama Mae keeps the garden for us. She likes to come and check on us, because she thinks my Mom doesn't know how to take care of people. She also tries to make me and Trane work in the garden, and we try to get out of it because the garden is itchy, and the bugs are gross.

"Hurry up, Billie," said Eutreece. "We have to get there before the boys come out."

This was unusual for Eutreece to be hurrying me. But I had a lot to think about, with this new cousin. "They know where we're going to be," I said.

"No they don't." And instead of going over the boards to Surveillance Place, she started through the weeds and muck toward the canal.

"Hey!" I said, "I've got new sneakers!"

But I followed her down to our rowboat, stepping carefully. The boat was half sunk.

"It's full of water," I said, "Nobody put the plastic sheet over it!"

"Don't look at me," said Eutreece. "I haven't been in this boat in weeks."

I had a feeling that Trane and I had been out in the boat last, so I changed the subject. "I guess we have to bail it out."

"No time," said Eutreece. "The potato heads will be here soon." She got right into the boat, and of course it sank farther into the water.

I had to push off, and I tried to do it and jump into my seat and also keep my sneakers dry, which didn't work very well at all. I put my feet up on the seat. "You row," I told her. "My mom will kill me if I ruin the sneakers."

My mother goes bananas if you mess up new stuff. It's bizarre, because she always says, "Material things don't matter." Then she throws a fit if you get a speck of dirt on the floor or mud on your new sneakers. It seems to me that if you aren't materialistic, then you shouldn't care if material things get dirty.

In this case, though, I was on her side, because I was thinking of—just maybe—visiting my cousin, and I didn't want to go in muddy sneakers.

Eutreece rowed straight across the canal. It only takes about four strokes, and she gave one last big one that shoved us into the weeds.

She got out and pulled us up a little more, and then I carefully swung my feet over so I missed the water—and sank right into mud up to my ankles. "My shoes are ruined, Eutreece. I might just as well forget it!"

"Shh! You can wash your shoes," she said. "We have to be quiet now, we don't know who's here. We have to sneak."

Eutreece is a genius of sneaking. She can hold perfectly still for so long you almost forget it's a human girl there. Meanwhile my whole self was sweating and itching and feeling muddy water squelch in my formerly new sneakers.

There was a flat area between us and the warehouse. This side of warehouse is as blank as a piece of paper, and there wasn't anybody over here anyhow, but we still froze for a long time while Eutreece looked one way, then the other. Then we ran for the building. I ran so fast that I slammed up against the wall and stung my hands. We held ourselves flat to the wall and waited. Then Eutreece pointed with her chin. She wanted to go around the corner to the pile of barrels and metal that you can see from Surveillance Place.

We sneaked around the corner, along the wall, and we sneaked around the pile of metal drums and engine parts.

"Okay," I said. "Where?"

"Shh!" said Eutreece. "Keep your voice down. Look for disturbed earth. It was right beside this big fan thing. Look!"

And there was a little pile of dirt right next to all the metal junk. And next to the pile of dirt was a hole.

"That's it." We squatted down.

"It's a hole."

"He must have changed his mind and dug it up."

"Unless he never buried it in the first place."

"I saw it, Billie."

"Well, I know you saw something. Maybe it was a dead fish and some raccoons came and dug it up for dinner."

She gave me a look.

"Why not? That makes as much sense as what you said!"

"He had a Bargain Bob bag," she said, "and when he left, he didn't have it."

"Well, there's nothing in the hole," I said.

19

"Shh!" she whispered. "Something is going on, and we have to find out what it is." I was about to say, "Why do we have to find out?" but she said, "We'll climb the barrels and look inside the warehouse."

I didn't get the connection, but I'd always wanted to climb the barrels. That's what I'm like: I like to be doing, so I started up the metal pyramid. The pile went up to some windows about where the second floor should be. The motors and barrels were all big and sturdy looking, but it was a challenge to climb them just the same. The first layer was easy, but the top barrel, the one you'd have to stand on to look in the window, was shaky. It wanted to roll. Eutreece was still on the ground. I gave her a wave to show I was okay, so she started to climb too, a lot slower than I had.

I looked out across the swamp and canal, and I was glad I was here spying instead of visiting some cousin I had to be on best behavior with. But I was supposed to be looking inside the warehouse. I waited till Eutreece was huffing and puffing up over the middle barrels before I climbed the shaky one. It had a big hole in the middle where it had rusted through, so I stood on the rim. Then I twisted my body around and put my elbows on the sill of the window and lifted myself on my arms and tiptoes till I could see in, but just barely.

There was no glass in the panes, but there was some on the window sill, so I had to be careful where I put my arms. Inside was a huge empty room with a couple of tipped-over chairs and a burned place on the floor like someone had once built a fire.

All of a sudden, something came at me through the air, right at my face, and I yelled and jumped backward. Just as I was losing my balance, I realized it was birds flying in and out of the warehouse, but it was too late to get my balance back.

"What!" yelled Eutreece, but I couldn't answer because I was rocking from side to side on the shaky barrel, and my leg had started slipping into the hole. I pulled it out just in time, but then I really started to fall and only caught myself by jumping down to the next barrel, only that's where Eutreece's hands were and she yelled because I'd stepped on her finger, and she started slipping, and I was half slipping and half jumping, and one barrel tipped and another one shook, and the first one started to roll, and Eutreece and I sort of slid and jumped and scrambled until we were down. I took one last really big leap and hit the ground running. The falling barrel banged behind us. We ran for the weeds as fast as we could. Eutreece glides really fast for someone who is almost fat, and I ran even faster, around the corner and into the weeds. We splashed our way to the boat and pushed off. This time I rowed. I thought I was going to break the oars I rowed so hard. We looked behind us at the canal where we had made a clear place in the slimy green stuff. We didn't talk till we were across the canal.

"What did you see?" she asked. "Who was in there?"

"Birds," I said.

"Birds?"

"Yeah, I lost my balance because all of a sudden these birds started flying at me."

"You mean we about broke our necks running from *some birds*?"

"They came right at my face."

"Billie!"

"There had been people in there sometime. It looked like someone built a fire once a long time ago."

"But there was nothing to run from!"

21

"You're the one who ran, Eutreece! I almost fell, and you ran, and I ran after you."

"You stepped on my hand!"

"Sorry."

When we were back inside Surveillance Place she took her usual spot in the best chair and I took my usual spot in the not-best chair. She kept shaking her head. "You just started jumping off the barrels and stepping on my hand and making all that noise and there wasn't even anybody there!"

"Listen, Eutreece, I was the one up there exposing myself to danger, and this bird came at me and I thought it was a bat or something, and it made me lose my balance and I almost fell and broke my neck! And the whole thing was your idea in the first place. I didn't want to go over there anyhow."

"Yes you did," said Eutreece, shaking her head. "Something is going down over there. Neighbor buried something and then he changed his mind and dug it up. You don't bury something if it's legal. We have to go spy on Neighbor."

"No," I said. "We're almost teenagers," I said, "We're too old for spy stuff."

"I guess *you* have better things to do."

"What's that supposed to mean?"

"Like going to visit your no-color cousin."

"Good grief, Eutreece! People can't help what color they are!"

"That's right, and you're not that color."

"I'm half that color."

"Half of nothing is nothing, and you're not no-color."

I was just getting geared up for a real argument with her, when I felt something on my leg: my nice light tan smooth leg with little light hairs just the same color, and now there was this thick trickle of blood creeping down it.

Eutreece noticed too, and said, "I hope you didn't get that on a rusty nail."

"Why? What about rusty nails?"

She opened up the big round tin can we keep in Surveillance Place. It used to have Christmas popcorn in it, and it had a design of snow and sleighs. We use it for things we don't want to get damp or eaten by swamp rats. She got me a tissue and said, "Rusty nails give you tetanus, also known as lockjaw. Aunt Lucy said people used to get it Down South from running around barefoot and stepping on sharp things. It's a terrible disease. Your back tightens up the wrong way, and your mouth freezes in this ugly grin and won't open."

"You're making that up."

"Go ahead and don't believe me."

"When do you know if you got it?"

"It could be weeks," she said.

Eutreece has tons of awful stories of what used to happen Down South that she gets from Aunt Lucy who is like a hundred and seven years old.

On the other hand, Eutreece also reads a lot of books about science.

"So what's the cure?" I said, thinking about how she told me if you get rabies you have to take twenty-nine needles the size of rulers in your belly all at once.

Eutreece shook her head sadly. "I'm sorry to say there's no cure."

"There's no cure!"

"Not once you start to tighten up. They say it helps to make the cut bleed, though."

It was already bleeding a lot, but I fooled with the cut so it bled more. "There's no way to know if you got it?"

Eutreece shook her head slow and sad. "You just go on about your life, and then one day when you least expect it, Whomp! Back goes your head, like the bow from a bow and arrow, and—say your prayers."

In my mind, I told myself: Eutreece exaggerates. Eutreece makes things up. The rabies thing turned out to be five needles, not twenty-nine, and they were just normal-sized needles and not even all at once. Out loud, I said, "Well, if I'm going to die anyway, I think I may just go visit my cousin. Maybe I'll go visit her and then I'll bring her back for the Fish Fry."

"Not to my Fish Fry," said Eutreece.

"Your father said I can invite any of my friends and family."

"I don't want no Ugly Cousin at my Fish Fry."

"Well, maybe I don't want you in my Surveillance Place!"

"Whose Surveillance Place?"

And we were staring at each other like a real fight was about to happen when we heard an unusual sound like tiny whispering in the middle of the shifting reeds. Eutreece and I looked at each other, and the fight was over, and our eyes had one of our private conversations.

Our eyes said: *Do you hear it?*

I hear it too.

Get a weapon.

We picked up the broomsticks that prop open the canal side window. We stood on either side of the blanket door and raised the sticks. Whatever came through the door was going to get smashed on the head.

It seemed like forever before something happened. My mind kept saying, *Come on, come on, get it over with!* And then the blanket bulged.

Someone was coming in, and we smacked hard and high, above our own heads, where a man would be. But we only smacked blanket, and it ripped off, and covered up the person, who started screaming a kid scream.

Trane and Martin were standing outside the door, so it had to be Hector Hernandez we had knocked down.

Martin started to back away, but Eutreece yelled, "Martin Robinson! Get your retarded little self right back here!"

Meanwhile, I was trying to untangle Hector from the blanket, but he kept yelling and kicking and tangling himself even worse.

"Hector," I said, "it's Billie!"

He kicked some more.

"Hector! Stop it! It's just us! You're lucky you didn't all three get your heads bashed in!"

Eutreece pulled Martin and Trane inside. I finally got Hector untangled and he was crying and rubbing his face.

We made the three boys sit in a row on the floor.

"Now," said Eutreece, sitting back down in her lounge chair and crossing her arms over her chest. "Just exactly what did you little street rat bird brains think you were doing?"

I said, "Bird brains is a compliment to these jerks. I'd say cockroach brains."

Hector whimpered, "Trane, your sister hit me!"

"Yeah, Billie," said Trane. "You hit Hector? That's child abuse."

I lifted my broomstick like I might hit Trane too.

Eutreece leaned down so her face was close to the boys. She grabbed the two outside heads and pressed them against the middle head, which happened to be Martin. "Child abuse is nothing compared to what you three are going to get if you don't tell us what you were doing."

Martin's eyes got huge. Hector was sucking in his tears and snot and trying to look dangerous so nobody would remember he had cried. Trane said, "We were spying on you!"

Eutreece leaned back a little and looked down over her cheeks at the boys. She shook her head slowly. She looked at me. I shook my head slowly. Eutreece said, "Don't ever, ever do that again. *We* are the spies. You can be our assistant spies, *if* we *request* assistance. But don't ever sneak up on us again."

We let them assist by cleaning out Surveillance Place. They emptied the crumbs out of the Christmas popcorn can and swept the floor and wiped off the chairs. Eutreece and I hung the blanket door back up. Eutreece and I pretended that we hadn't almost had a fight, and I didn't think about tetanus lockjaw again until almost bedtime.

Chapter Four
Family Stuff

Daddy didn't come to dinner that night, so we stayed quiet. Parker kept making faces and squealing, but the rest of us never have much to say when Daddy's sick. When he's not sick, we don't even think about it. I don't think about things that make me unhappy, like when we were all separated. Sometimes I think back to before he got sick, when he and Mom and Trane and I lived in an apartment, and there was a lot of noise and music and parties and people in and out.

There were fights, too. But I don't think about that.

Except when Daddy's sick, and I start remembering all the bad things.

I remember one really big fight about how you pronounce a word. The word was just plain old "Aunt" like Aunt Lucy at the Robinson's house. My mom said Daddy pronounced it like he was trying to sound Upper Class, and Daddy said my mom pronounced it like a little bug at the picnic. They started out joking, but I think they had had a little bit too much wine with dinner, and they started getting louder and louder and after a while they started saying bad things to each other that didn't have

27

anything at all to do with anyone's Aunt. Trane and I went in the other room and turned the TV up real loud.

After that fight, Daddy left and didn't come home, and Mom cried and he still didn't come home, and after a couple of days we didn't have any milk in the refrigerator. That was when she packed me and Trane, and we went to live at Mama Mae's. We didn't see Daddy until almost the end of the year, and when he did come to see us he was walking with a cane. But he got a lot better when we were all staying at Mama Mae's, and while we were there, he carved himself a beautiful new cane shaped like a snake. Now, even when he isn't walking right, he still looks fine because of that cane. So he and our Mom worked it out together, and we moved to our two-tone blue home on Fish House Lane. That was two years ago, and one year ago, Baby Parker came.

Mostly everything is just fine, even if it's quieter than it was in our old apartment or even at Mama Mae's house. And Daddy is almost okay, except maybe he grunts a little bit when his joints hurt. And sometimes he takes long naps in his studio. I don't think about those old fighting days, or about the year with Mama Mae. I'm a person who keeps my mind as well as my body on the move, and I like to go really fast over the bad things. I don't think about emergency rooms or broken families or fighting or lockjaw.

We had a quiet dinner of bread and salade Niçoise, which means with tuna fish and olives along with the usual salad stuff. Trane made faces at Parker, and Mom didn't seem unhappy, just thinking. I volunteered to wash dishes because it kept me moving, and after the dishes were done, when the bad thoughts started to slip in again, I ran out to the porch to make sure my good sneakers were drying without stains. Trane played with Parker, and I helped Mom fold the clean laundry. Then she and Trane had a discussion about bedtimes in the summer, and he finally went upstairs. Then Parker cried, and then Mom fed Parker and he stopped crying and went to sleep, and then it got really quiet.

It got so quiet that I started thinking about bad things again, and I thought about what if Daddy had to go to the emergency room, and also my back felt just a little tight.

I went through the living room to the little den we call Daddy's studio. It only has space for a daybed for when he's too tired to go upstairs. I could see the bottom half of him. He was lying on his back on the bed with his arms straight down beside him on top of the covers. I didn't mean to bother him, I just wanted to be near him. I moved into the doorway so I could see his face too. His eyes were closed, and his arms were dark with curves like carved wood.

Sometimes it's like my Daddy can see when his eyes are closed. One of his hands twitched and his beautiful deep voice said, "Darling Billie, is that you?"

"I didn't mean to wake you, Daddy."

He didn't open his eyes, but he turned over the hand that had twitched for me to hold.

"What up, Baby Girl?"

There is something about his strong warm hand, and his voice like a cello that always makes me tell him the truth. So when I said, "Oh, I'm just in a grumpy mood," I knew it was true, and of course right away I felt better.

He smiled with his eyes closed. "That's okay," he said. "That's just a mood. Everybody has moods. They have brown moods and red moods and blue moods and moody blues. Moods change," he said, and I knew that was true too. We held hands a while, and then his hand relaxed, and I knew he was going off to sleep, so I let him alone.

I was going to go up to my room when I saw Mom coming with the laundry basket of clean clothes. "Bedtime?" she said.

Usually I would have started some kind of discussion about how she treats me like a little kid, but I was still under the influence of telling Daddy the truth, so I said, "I don't think I can go to sleep."

She said, "Do you want me to sing to you?"

When I was small, I used to love her sad folk songs. She would lie in bed beside me and sing me those songs and I would see what was happening in the songs on the wall, like a movie, only better because it was being projected just for me.

I pointed at my leg and said, "I got a cut."

She put down the laundry basket and crouched next to me, touched the skin beside the cut. The blood had dried now, and it was crusty and ugly. "Let's go upstairs to the bathroom and clean it up."

The bathroom is nice and cool at night because it has a big screened window. You can see the elevated highway up above and little car lights, but we are so far away that we don't need curtains. My mom sat me on the rim of the bathtub. She ran the water and hummed one of her songs and got a washcloth and wiped off my leg, starting at the knee and working down.

After a while, I said, "Mommy, did you ever hear of lockjaw?"

She dabbed the water away with a soft towel. "Sure, I've heard of lockjaw. Its other name is tetanus. You get it from puncture wounds. You get it from something sharp that was deep in the dirt where the tetanus bug lives. It has to puncture deep into you for you to get it. This is just

30

a surface cut. Besides, you kids got your tetanus shots before we ever moved out here."

"You mean I'm like inoculated?"

"I think you may have to get a booster shot in a couple of years, but you're fine for now. You don't have to worry about this cut."

"Why don't people tell you what you're safe from and what you still have to watch out for?"

She grunted. She was lining up three band aids side-by-side, just the right way.

Well, I thought, that's one thing I don't have to worry about. Almost like magic I could feel my eye lids getting heavy. I let her put her arm around my shoulder and walk me back to bed. My mom smells like bread rising. I even let her sit beside me on the bed and sing one of her totally weird folk songs where the hero kills the girl and then everyone gets all sad because he gets hung! And she complains about violence in today's music.

I was letting myself sink down into sleep, but I came up for a second. I said, "Hey, Mom, I think I will go visit that cousin. For just one night, though. I have to be back for the Robinson Family Fish Fry."

She gave me a big hug and said she was so glad, and I let her hug me and went to sleep and had good dreams about swimming that turned into flying, and I flew over and under all the bridges and elevated highways. It could take your breath away.

Chapter Five
The White Side

It was already hot and sticky when I got up the next day, and my mom told me that she had called Aunt Barbara, who is really Cousin Barbara, and it was all arranged. They were coming to pick me up today.

I wasn't sure I was happy that she had gone ahead and planned all this without me, and I was going to complain, but I saw Daddy in the kitchen. He was not only out of bed, he was looking great in a white tee shirt that showed off his smooth dark skin. *And* he was stirring up French chef crêpes, which is pancakes that are so thin you can see through them. That is, if you can stand not eating them long enough to look! His snake-cane was lying way over beside the door like he didn't even need it today.

Daddy used to be a cook to earn money when he was an artist, and his crêpes are the best. We smear them with jam or peanut butter or honey, and sometimes we smear on all three at once. We were still eating when Mama Mae come driving up Fish House Lane in her huge black Cadillac car that is older than I am. My Daddy calls it the Barge of the Nile, and it belonged to Daddy Joe, who died before I was born. He had just retired from being a transit worker to become a full-time preacher when he died.

Mama Mae told us the whole story of his death and his funeral and the three preachers at the funeral and what they ate after his funeral. She doesn't want me and Trane to feel like we missed anything. Her stories are pretty interesting, but they always have a lesson. She's a retired school teacher, and if she doesn't have anything else to teach you, she works on your grammar.

She was bringing plants to set out in our garden. She had on a whole gardening outfit including a hat decorated with butterflies and matching gloves and a green blouse and cropped green pants and gardening clogs. Trane and I went out to help carry, but she gave the box to Trane and just stood there looking me up and down from top to bottom. Then I remembered I was still wearing my nightgown.

"Billie," she said, "I know you just got up, because if you got up an hour ago or even fifteen minutes ago, you would be wearing clothes."

"Yes ma'am," I said. Most of the time that's enough, just to be respectful. Especially now that I don't live in her house. "I just came down to say good morning and now I'm going to go get dressed." I don't believe in lying, but Mama Mae knew as well as I did that I'd been up awhile, especially when she went inside and saw everyone around the table waiting for the next *crêpe* off the griddle.

Daddy gave her a kiss, and she fussed about him working up a sweat, and then Mom brought Baby Parker for her to kiss, and then Mama Mae said she had eaten but she might just have one of those crêpes.

Meanwhile, I sneaked upstairs and put on my best-fitting shorts that are tight but comfortable. I took my time, thinking about this strange cousin and her swimming pool and what Mama Mae would say when she heard I was going to go visit them. We used to go to the public pool near her house, and she would always go with us with a big hat and bags of food because she didn't trust the kind of children who went to the public pools. We were a lot younger then, but she is still extremely particular about what we eat and who we eat with.

I gave my hair a good brushing and clipped it at the back of my neck and got my sandals. Then I went down and had some more crêpes. Trane had gone out back to give water to Panther, and they were talking about Daddy's health when I came down. I know that was the subject because they stopped talking when I came in, and my mom started telling Mama Mae about how I was going to go visit the cousins who lived in a place called Pinnacle Estates.

Mama Mae wanted to know if I had the right clothes, and Mom said it was just for overnight, and Mama Mae made a noise that meant my mom didn't get the point. I cleared the table, and Mama Mae and Mom did the breakfast dishes, and Daddy played with Parker, and Trane came back in, and it was just like a commercial: we were the happy family that purchased the product.

And then a car honked.

Mama Mae lifted her eyebrows, which means, *Somebody has no manners,* because one of her rules is that you don't honk, you knock. But another one of her rules is *Think before you speak,* so she only used her eyebrows.

"Holy Moley!" yelled Trane. "It's a Mercedes Benz in my front yard!"

I couldn't help myself. I ran to the door too. Our turnaround is the very end of Fish House Lane. At this moment, in the turnaround were: our old station wagon, Mama Mae's Barge of the Nile, and a silver Mercedes Benz. It was almost as long as the Barge but much, much newer. The engine was running like it was ready for a quick getaway, and a woman was standing between the car and the house like she didn't know which way to turn. I had a glimpse of someone in the front seat, but that person ducked its head down when we came out.

The woman was pretty tan for a white person, and she was wearing an actual, real life short-skirted white tennis dress.

Mom came out carrying Parker. "It's Barbara!" she cried. "Oh, Barbara!"

And right away the woman in the tennis outfit started waving and talking. She and Mom met halfway, and they hugged and had trouble reaching each other because of Parker, and Parker tried to grab Barbara's earrings.

She was saying how she knew they were early, but she had gone out early for tennis, and when she went home Celia was ready, so they said, "Why not," and here they were! And then it was how Mom hadn't changed a bit and Barbara hadn't changed a bit, and so on. Meanwhile, Mama Mae was getting all stiff because nobody was doing proper introductions. They were just standing there gabbing like they were the only people in the world.

Meanwhile, here came Eutreece and Martin and Little Bit Robinson. Of course they had seen the car and wanted to know who was in it. They didn't come all the way to the house, though. They stopped out beyond the cars.

Mom finally remembered her manners and introduced Barbara to Mama Mae and Daddy and me and Trane. We were supposed to call her Aunt Barb, even though she was a cousin. She said, "I don't know what got into Celia! She refuses to get out of the car! I guess she thinks the world is supposed to be air-conditioned!"

Mama Mae was frowning with her eyes and lifting her chin. This was her way of looking at badly behaved children. Daddy calls it the Hairy Eyeball. He and Mama

Mae love each other a lot, but as best I can tell, Daddy was not always well-behaved when he was a child.

He smiled his sweet, handsome smile with a little bit of sharp under it and said to Aunt Barb, "I understand you're planning to treat Billie to some air conditioning. Sort of the opposite of a Fresh Air Camp, I guess."

Mama Mae didn't think his joke was very polite either. So she gave *him* the Hairy Eyeball.

But Aunt Barb laughed and laughed. Her hands waved in the air like flags. "Oh, we just want the cousins to get to know each other! We're so glad Billie decided to come."

I wished Eutreece hadn't heard it, but she did. She had moved closer to the cars, and I saw her cross her arms over her chest. She looked at me and jerked her chin towards the Surveillance Place. But I shook my head No.

Meanwhile, Trane and Martin ran over to the Mercedes Benz.

Aunt Barb screamed, "Celia! Can't you get out of the car and come and meet your cousins?"

Mom said, "Maybe the kids are scaring her."

"Oh," said Aunt Barb, "Celia isn't timid. I mean, not usually."

I didn't like the way Mama Mae wasn't saying anything and my mom was jabbering at the same time as Aunt Barb and especially the way Eutreece had gone over and leaned herself on the Mercedes Benz. Suddenly, she looked disgusted and walked off. I figured she was heading off to Surveillance Place without me.

"Celia!" cried Aunt Barb. "Come out and meet your cousins! Little boy," she said to Martin Robinson, "would you go open the car door?"

"He's not her cousin!" said Trane. "I am!"

"Oh," said Aunt Barb. "Well, then, you open it, darling."

Trane and Martin pulled each other's hands off the car door to get to do it first.

Mom said, "Don't make her come out if she doesn't want to—"

Now, Mama Mae can't stand the way Mom believes in convincing kids instead of making them. So Mama Mae whispered, "*Children* deciding what to do? I don't know about that."

Daddy laughed.

"I'm sorry for the way Celia's behaving," said Aunt Barb. "I don't know—she's not usually like this!"

Mama Mae looked Aunt Barb in the eye and said, "I'm sure your child has a great deal of potential. I'm a retired school teacher, and I know that however a child behaves, he has potential." Then she sat down on the glider next to Daddy with her garden trowel in her hand.

Aunt Barb said, "Celia really wants Billie to come over. You should have heard her in the car. You wouldn't believe how bored she gets once school is out, and she doesn't go to camp for another two weeks—"

Mom said everyone is a little shy in a new situation.

"But she's not!" cried Aunt Barb. "That's the point! She loves to perform! She takes three dance classes a week! Or she used to. Celia!"

A hat and sunglasses surfaced in the car. It was a black, floppy hat. Trane and Martin Robinson had opened the car door, but *Wham!*—it slammed back again.

Trane called, "I don't think she wants to come out."

Mom said, "Let's go inside and have tea. We'll give her time, and I bet she'll change her mind."

Daddy said, "Let me whip you up some crêpes."

And of course Barbara said No, no she couldn't and more about how strange that Celia wasn't coming out, and Trane yelled how he could still see her hat. And

Mama Mae said, "Please excuse me," she had some gardening to do, and went around the back.

Mom said, "Trane, you watch the car, okay?"

Eutreece hadn't come back, so I figured she was going to say I betrayed her or went back on my word, or something. I wasn't so sure I liked this adventure anymore anyhow, what with how Celia was hiding and Aunt Barb squealing and Mama Mae and Eutreece both walking off on us.

Mom and the baby and Aunt Barb went in, and Daddy used my shoulder for balance, just for a second. Aunt Barb turned down the crêpes, but she did accept a glass of Spicy Icy and a cookie. She wanted a tour of the house, she said. I was glad Mama Mae didn't hear her, because Mama Mae says you should never ask to look at people's stuff or sit on their beds. We went into the living room which is also Mom's workroom. It is full of rolls of cloth and Daddy's totem-pole people. Mom uses them to model her robes and turbans.

I was pretty sure that our house looked funny to Aunt Barb. She kept saying things like, "Well, isn't that unusual!" She went to the window and saw Mama Mae and the vegetable garden and the marsh, and the highway. "Oh!" she said. "What an unusual view. Does it get noisy with all the cars overhead?"

"It's the quietest place we've ever lived," said Daddy.

We went back in the kitchen, and Aunt Barb was thrilled to find out how healthy the cookies were with oatmeal and sunflower seeds and sweet potatoes and molasses and hardly any oil at all. She wished Celia would come in and try these. Celia never ate anything except junk food. "Such a difference, her and her brother," said Aunt Barb. "He is a gourmet eater. He critiques every meal we eat. He collects restaurant reviews! He's in

Europe, did I tell you? He's in Europe and Richie had to go to California, and Celia and I are just rattling around the house all alone." Then she started in about Celia again. "I don't know what got into Celia. She never hid in the car like that. She used to love to perform. Do you take dance, Billie?"

"I like basketball better."

"An athlete!" cried Aunt Barb. "Of course, you look very athletic. You're more developed than Celia too. I bet you like to swim. I hope you'll get Celia into the pool. The kids hardly use it anymore."

She and my Mom kept blabbing. Very softly, Daddy said, "Do you really want to go, Darling Billie?"

"I won't go if you don't want me to."

"I want you to have a good time," said Daddy. "And you should know your relatives on your mother's side."

"I don't think Mama Mae wants me to."

"She worries about people getting hurt," he said. "I don't want you to get hurt either."

"I won't get hurt!"

"I know you're a strong young lady."

And like always, when Daddy says something about me, I feel just how he says: I was a strong adventurer, all ready to meet the world! He is so handsome with his little beard under his chin and his crinkly sparkly eyes.

At that moment, someone screamed.

Everybody looked at each other in horror and headed for the door.

Aunt Barb waved her arms and screamed too: "Celia! Celia!" Celia had finally come out of the car, but she was standing on its hood. She was dressed all in black, a skinny girl wearing a long skirt and a floppy black hat. She was standing on the car making shrieks like a mouse.

The reason she was up there was because Black Panther was loose and wanted to play. Now I admit Panther would be scary if you didn't know her: she is as big as a pony and her tongue is about as long as her body. Also, she hadn't been loose yet today, so she was lurching and barking and howling with joy. Trane and Martin were making it worse by chasing her.

I said to Aunt Barb, "Don't worry, she's a very friendly dog. She just thinks Celia wants to play."

Aunt Barb cried, "Does it—bite?"

"Oh no," said my mother. "The worst danger is if she steps on you. Billie, hurry up! I don't know how she got loose."

Aunt Barb stopped screaming, but Cousin Celia kept on, every two seconds: *Eee! Eee!* It sounded fake to me.

When Panther saw me, she wagged her tail and made bigger circles around Aunt Barb's car. Trane and Martin started running bigger circles too. Panther made even bigger ones, and every two seconds Celia screamed: *Eee! Eee!*

Then I saw Eutreece come around the house with this look on her face that told me exactly who let Panther loose. I wondered if Mama Mae had seen her do it.

The dog leaped up in the air again trying to get to Celia. Maybe because Celia was dressed all in black, Panther thought they were long lost sisters or something. Celia scrambled up the windshield and squatted on the roof of the car. "Eee! Eee!" she said.

"She's just playing," I said. "She won't hurt you."

Celia's sunglasses stared at me from under her floppy black hat. "Eee! Eee!" she said.

I finally knew what Eutreece meant about white being no color, because Celia had the palest skin I ever saw. Aunt Barb was tanned, but Celia looked like she never

40

went out. She had just about the whitest, skinniest arms I ever saw.

Aunt Barb and my mom were still talking, of course, and Daddy had sat back down on the glider. Aunt Barb told my mother that Celia once had a traumatic experience with a schnauzer.

I tried a new tactic. I pretended to ignore Panther. I turned around and gave Eutreece a look so she would know I knew she had done it. Panther loped over and swiped me with her tongue, and I jumped sideways and grabbed her by the collar. "Bad girl!" I said, still looking at Eutreece. Eutreece gave me what I call her fat smile, which just stretches her lips and squeezes her eyes shut.

I dragged Panther to the back of the house. She really didn't want to get separated from all the fun again, but I managed to fasten her to the chain.

Mama Mae said, "What's all the ruckus about?"

"Oh nothing," I said. "Panther got loose and scared that girl. My cousin."

"Your cousin," said Mama Mae, twisting her mouth up. "I think that child needs to learn some manners."

"Yes ma'am," I said. But for once I agreed with her.

When I got back, Celia was still hunkered on the roof of her car, but she had stopped squeaking and pulled out a camera from somewhere. She took my picture as I walked toward her. I said, "I tied up the dog. I'm sorry she scared you. Do want some cookies and iced tea?"

Celia shook her head.

Aunt Barb called, "Celia! Be polite!"

"No thank yew!" she said in a prissy fake voice. "Are they chocolate chip?"

"Celia!" cried Aunt Barb.

I said, "They're sunflower seed and sweet potato."

Celia said, "Yuck."

41

I shrugged. "More for us, then."

She said, "Are you coming to my house?"

Eutreece was still standing at the edge of our property with a big No on her face, but I was mad at *her* now too. "By the way," I said, "those cookies are nutritious as well as delicious. And I think maybe I will come over." Eutreece's eyebrows dropped like a ton of bricks, and she turned away and marched off toward her house.

Well, to make a long story short, Celia never went in the house, but she did climb off the roof and get back in her car. I went inside and washed Panther off my hands and got my things together. Celia was totally weird, but I figured if worse came to worst, I could always call home and Mom would come and get me.

Mama Mae came in to check what I was packing. I took my sleeping tee with pink rabbits on it. I'm too old for bunny rabbits, but it was the only nightgown I had that didn't have holes. I had to take my old sneakers, though, because the new ones were still damp. Mom gave me a plastic bag to stuff things in, but Mama Mae said I couldn't take that, and went out to her car and came back with a canvas bag with a design of flowers and books on it. It was pretty nice, actually.

I kissed Mama Mae, Parker, Mom, and Daddy, but Trane was running around with Martin Robinson. Daddy said, "Have yourself a good time, baby."

And then I got in the silver Mercedes Benz with Celia and Aunt Barbara. I looked back and saw everyone on the porch waving and getting smaller. I had a funny feeling like instant homesickness, and I was only going away for one night.

As we drove down Fish House Lane, I saw Eutreece already up on her porch reading.

42

I didn't do anything wrong, I thought; *she* did. It's her fault for letting Panther loose and scaring my cousin.

Then she got smaller too, and it was like everything sort of faded away except the gray leather seats and air conditioned comfort of the silver Mercedes-Benz. And, of course, my cousin, Weird Celia.

Chapter Six
At Celia's

Celia sat in the back with me, knees and feet up on the seat, sunglasses staring at me while she sucked her lollipop and snapped pictures out the window. Aunt Barb did the talking, and she had whole lists of questions about my family. Mama Mae would go bananas over asking so much personal stuff. Luckily, she asked two or three questions at a time so I could pick out what I wanted to answer. For example, she asked, Did my Daddy have a job? How many of those African dresses could my mother make every week? Did we only eat health food? I chose the last one and told her about Mama Mae's organic vegetable garden.

Aunt Barb seemed perfectly happy getting one-third of her questions answered. "Did you hear that, Celia? They eat fresh vegetables every day! I wish you would even eat a nice salad once in a while. I'm always putting out salads, Billie, with crunchy croutons and slivered almonds, things a child ought to like, but not Celia! Celia turns up her nose at all the best food."

Celia photographed the back of her mother's head.

One of the advantages of having lived not only with my own family but also with Mama Mae was that I had learned you shouldn't be surprised by how different people are. For example, my mom believes kids should be convinced, so we spend a lot of time discussing things. But Mama Mae believes kids should do exactly what they're told when they're told or else. And Aunt Barb seemed to think you were only supposed to give your kid little hints. She kept saying, "Did you hear that, Celia? I think that's a good idea, don't you, Celia?"

Once we got off Fish House Lane and past the apartments where the Hernandezes live, and past my school and past some stores, and onto the highway, Aunt Barb finally quieted down.

Celia said her first word since we got in the car. "Do the kids at your school all carry concealed weapons?"

"Celia!" shrieked Aunt Barb.

If it had just been me and Celia, I would have made up a whole Legend of the 'Hood to scare her, but I was being a polite young lady, so I said, "Oh, no, nobody would ever dare carry a weapon in my school. Our principal would *excoriate* anyone who carried a weapon."

"Do you hear that, Celia?" said Aunt Barb. "Billie has an excellent vocabulary! Celia, are you listening? Wouldn't it be nice if you used your vocabulary like Billie does?"

Celia closed her eyes and made a snoring sound. The rest of the conversation consisted of Aunt Barb telling me the things that Celia used to do, like take dance lessons and tennis lessons and how she used to want to be a musical comedy star. It was pretty obvious that Aunt Barb missed the old Celia.

I kept thinking what I would tell Eutreece about these people, but then I remembered that Eutreece might never speak to me again, and I wondered if Weird Celia and her swimming pool were worth it.

45

Their neighborhood had its own name on a sign: Pinnacle Estates. Aunt Barbara explained that Pinnacle Estates is a gated community. They have their own special security, and everything is private, even the streets, so stray people can't come wandering in. The houses were huge and low to the ground with bushes in the shapes of basketballs and balloons. I didn't see a single kid on skates, scooter, skateboard, or bicycle.

I said, "If I lived here, I would ride my bike all the time."

"We have extra bikes," said Aunt Barb. "Celia, don't we have extra bikes in the garage? I don't know if they have air in the tires, though."

"I don't do bikes," said Celia. "I drive sports cars."

The bushes at Celia's house were shaped like lollipops. We pulled up the driveway, and the garage door opened silently then closed behind us. We stepped from the car to the dim garage up a little step into the kitchen. The car had been air conditioned, but the house was like a giant refrigerator. It was awesome. Eutreece would love it, because she hates the heat, but my dad would have had to wear a sweater. My mom would have said, "You could run a Third World country on the electricity this air conditioner is using!"

As soon as we got in the house, Celia disappeared, so Aunt Barb gave me a tour, and I didn't care what Mama Mae thought, I wanted to see every detail.

The enormous living room had everything in the exact same pale cream color: carpet, couches, chairs, and walls. The dining room had a wall-sized cabinet full of dishes imported from Italy and the biggest chandelier I ever saw in real life. We looked at the game room and the bathrooms and the laundry room and the maid's room, but just for a second, because they actually had a maid, and her stuff was in there. She was having a day off. Then we looked at the master bedroom with its own bathroom and room-sized closet and the other bedrooms, and we finished at Celia's room.

Celia was lying on one of her two beds. The quilts were black and white striped, and the room was crowded with red, white, and black silk flowers and framed posters and a vanity table with an upholstered bench.

"Very sophisticated," I said, "but congenial too." I was trying to keep up the advanced vocabulary that Aunt Barb liked.

"We just redid it. Celia was tired of pink." Celia did that little fake snore again. She was lying back on the bed all spread out with her black stretch skirt looking like it was going to rip. "Well," said Aunt Barb, "I'll leave you girls here to get better acquainted!"

I said, "Oh, Aunt Barb, I'd like to see outside too!"

"Do you mean the deck? Celia, show Billie the deck while I get us something to eat—"

I said, "Don't you think we ought to do some exercise before we eat." They weren't getting my hints. Celia stared up at the ceiling. So I just said right out, "Like swimming!"

"What a wonderful idea!" cried Aunt Barb. "You two go swimming! Celia, get your cousin a bathing suit!"

"I brought my own," I said.

Celia said, "I don't want to swim. The water has yellow worms."

"It's just the trees dropping their—"

"Worms," said Celia.

"Leaves!" said Aunt Barbara. "It's just leafy things. It is *not* worms."

"I don't care," I said. "I'll swim anyhow."

Aunt Barb went out, talking as she went. "Now you girls go for a swim! No lunch till you've been swimming!" She didn't wait to see if Celia got *that* hint.

Celia immediately hopped off the bed and closed the door behind her mother. "I hate sports," said Celia, "and I hate exercise."

"I thought you took three dance classes."

"That was a million years ago. I gave that up, but my mother is in denial. Do you want to see my stuff?"

The best thing about someone like Celia is that you can just say what you want. So I said, "No, actually your mother showed me plenty of stuff already. I want to swim."

"*My* stuff is interesting."

I said, "Where's the bathroom? I want to put on my bathing suit."

She pointed to a wall of mirrors, and I saw door handles on different mirrors. I opened one, and it was a closet. I opened another one, and it was closets too. Celia didn't help me, but I didn't give up. The third door was her private bathroom.

This turned out to be just about my favorite thing about her house, not counting the pool, of course. Celia's bathroom was dark green. It had green tiles on the floor and up the walls and in the shower, which had not one, not two, but *four* shower heads! The toilet was green, and the sink, the bath mat, the cover for the toilet seat lid, the towels and wash cloths—all dark green. I mean, our bathroom at home is nice. It has a window with a view and it has seashell decorations, and it's actually bigger than Celia's. But however unique our bathroom is, we only have that one for all of us, and Celia's bathroom is just Celia's. No little brother pounding on the door to come in and pee while you're in the tub. And we don't even have a shower! Daddy talked about building a special outdoor shower for the summer, but he hasn't gotten around to it yet. In Celia's bathroom, you could curl up and sleep, like in your own green cave.

My suit was tight because it was last year's, but nothing was going to stop me from swimming. When I came out, Celia had put on her bathing suit too. Black, of course. She was totally straight up and down with no breasts or waist at all.

I said, "The labels are still on your swimsuit."

"I'm not going in."

"*I* am!"

Celia said, "Do you want to see something interesting?" She opened a drawer in her red bureau. Neatly arranged in this drawer was a whole set of *Nightmare on Elm Street* and *Halloween* movies. She also had books about *Nightmare on Elm Street* and pictures of various horror killers and toy razor claws. "I used to be so into that stuff," she said. "That's like my childhood in the drawer. When I was really small, I was terrified of everything. Then I internalized my fears and became one of the dangerous ones."

I said, "Cool."

She closed that drawer, and opened another one full of vampire stuff with black candles and velvet capes. She said, "These are my Satanic Obsession drawers. Do you want to see my Wicca drawers? Wicca is the religion of the witches, but it is totally separate from the Satanic Obsession stuff."

I said, "Actually, I'd like to go swimming now."

"I'll show you my brother's room later. I know the combination lock on his trunk. That's where he keeps his sex orgy devices."

I was afraid that if I didn't react more, she was going to keep showing me things till I did. So I said, "You're a regular pervert, aren't you?"

She smiled a little and shrugged, like that was all she wanted.

After I called her a pervert, things got surprisingly normal. She clipped back her stringy brown hair, and she let me tear off the labels on her bathing suit. We went outside on the deck beside the pool, but she refused to go in the water till we had skimmed off every one of the little yellow fuzzy things that the trees dropped. Celia seemed more obsessed by them than she was about vampires and Satan. We spent a lot time skimming the pool and sweeping the deck.

Next to the pool was a little house with stacks of tangerine-colored towels that were only for the pool. I loved this little house with its own shower and refrigerator. I figured I could live happily right in this house and go to school and come home and swim every day, especially if I could have Eutreece with me. Celia opened the refrigerator and asked me if I wanted a beer.

I said, "What do you do for fun when there's no one around to shock?"

"I get very bored," said Celia. "That's why you're here."

"That's why *you* think I'm here. I'm really here to go swimming!"

And I finally did. I walked in from the shallow end, just me, not a single other person, because Celia had dropped onto a lounge chair and wrapped herself in a cocoon of tangerine-colored towels.

I had never been in a pool before that wasn't full of other kids splashing and whistles blowing. I walked in slowly, hardly disturbing the water at all. Up to my waist, up to my neck. It was cool and blue and calm, and it held me up. It was as if the water and I were the same thing. I almost didn't want to disturb the blueness. I walked deeper and deeper until it was up to my neck and my mouth. I walked right under the water. I could have stayed in there all day. I could have stayed for a week.

Slowly I swam across the pool and then back. I dived in the deep end, and I climbed up on a dolphin-shaped float. After a while, Celia unwrapped herself and came in too, sort of slipping in over the side. She got on the other dolphin.

I overturned myself on purpose, and then I overturned Celia. From then on, she squealed and laughed like a regular kid, or I should say, like a regular kid Trane's age. But we had a good time. We splashed each other, and we lay on top of the dolphins and rested and talked about baseball, which it turned out that Celia actually knew a lot about. And then we dumped each other all over again.

Aunt Barb came out and brought us a tray of egg salad sandwiches and big soft chocolate chip cookies. She said we would have pizza for an early dinner. Celia said she hated egg salad, but she ate the cookies. While we ate, Aunt Barb got on her cell phone and called Celia's dad. "It's so nice to see someone using this swimming pool!" she told him. "They're been having a great time in the pool, Richie! They're having lunch now. Celia hasn't been in that pool for months! And Billie is the smartest girl, you should hear her vocabulary."

Celia said, "Tell him if someone would clean up the tree worms, I might use the pool."

After we ate, we lay around and then went back in the pool again. Aunt Barb kept telling us to enjoy ourselves as long as we wanted.

And we did. Celia was pretty much willing to do anything I wanted. Without her glasses and long black clothes, she was just an underdeveloped, goofy girl that was like a friend I'd had for a long time. Not my best friend, but a pretty good friend.

Once, when we were floating on the dolphins, looking up at the trees and sky, I said, "Trane would love to swim here."

"Bring him tomorrow," said Celia.

"You have to visit us first."

"Why?"

"It has to be fair. I visit, then you visit. Besides, you have to meet Eutreece."

"Who's that, the fat one who brought the dog to chase me?"

"She's not fat! She's solid as a tree."

"She's scary looking," said Celia.

"She was jealous about me coming to visit you." I decided not to say anything about Eutreece not liking white people very well. I said, "Her little brother is Trane's best friend and their baby is our baby's best friend."

Celia said, "I wish there were more people around here. It's very boring. I never used to notice because I was always taking my classes and getting tutored, but I went on strike from all after-school activities. My friends went to camp, and my brother took off for Europe. I tried to talk them into letting me go too, but he wanted to go alone to see all the dirty pictures and go to the bars. The only kids left around here are ones who don't like me. I'm too weird for them."

"You certainly are too weird."

She started to giggle and then waved her legs in the air.

So I waved my legs in the air, and then we had a leg wrestle, and played around some more, and dumped each other off the dolphins. She told me her mother gets totally phobic if Bianca is off when her dad is away on business.

"Who's Bianca?"

"She's the housekeeper. When Bianca's here, Mom goes off and does her shopping and tennis, and Bianca cleans, and I do what I want in my room. But when Bianca has a day off, my mother thinks she has to interact with me. It's bizarre. It's like she only worries about me when Bianca's off. But it's even worse now because my dad is away too. That's why we called you."

I said, "You and your mom both should come to the Robinsons' Welcome to Summer party." I had this idea that I would make Celia and Eutreece be friends, and Celia would get less weird and Eutreece would stop being jealous and hating the white side, and I could have both my sides and everything would be just as fine as I felt right now. "And if your mom doesn't want to stay late, you can sleep over," I said. "That way you can stay as late as the party goes, and your mom won't have to worry about you at all."

"Okay," said Celia. She didn't even think it over; she seemed that bored with her life.

We swam until the shadows got long and Aunt Barb told us she had ordered pizza. She had put on this lounge dress with puffy sleeves and pink and red roses. She had the kind of slippers with little heels and no backs and the front of each slipper was a red rose that matched the dress.

I had to put back on my same shorts, but Celia had a nice blue knit pants outfit. I wondered if Mama Mae would count a lounge outfit as clothes or pajamas.

53

We ate pizza and had ice cream, and Aunt Barb and I talked about child rearing.

After a while—maybe because I was on such good behavior around Aunt Barb—I had a funny feeling of homesickness. It wasn't real homesickness, like you want to call your mother and have her come and get you, but I kept thinking about home.

So I said, "Aunt Barb, I invited Celia to the big party on Fish House Lane on Saturday. It's the Robinsons' Welcome to Summer Fish Fry, and everyone is invited. I thought Celia could come and sleep over Saturday night, and you could come too."

Celia's eyes got big, like she hadn't meant for her mother to come. I hadn't really meant for Aunt Barb to come either, but now I did. Aunt Barb was very appreciative about being asked, and said she would think about it. Although she didn't think Celia ate fish.

I said there would be all kinds of food and probably no fish at all.

Celia said, "Since Bianca's off today, you could get her to stay Saturday night so you wouldn't be alone in the house."

I said, "Aunt Barb can sleep at our house too."

Aunt Barb laughed about that. "Oh, I almost never sleep away from my own bed," she said.

"She's phobic," said Celia.

"I'm not phobic! I just can't sleep if I don't know the place."

"She won't go in an airplane either."

"Celia!" cried Aunt Barb, but she didn't seem to be really mad.

After dinner, Aunt Barb got out a boxed set of classic Walt Disney movies: *Cinderella* and *Snow White* and of course *Beauty and the Beast* and *The Hunchback of Notre Dame* and all the rest.

"Mo-ther!" cried Celia. "Mo-ther! This is the most embarrassing thing you've ever done! Ever! You know I hate this kind of crap!"

Aunt Barb looked like she was about to cry, so I said Disney had always been my favorite, which wasn't true, but I felt bad for Aunt Barb. I chose *Beauty and the Beast*, and Celia lay on the floor on her back with her feet on the couch staring at the ceiling and snoring.

Aunt Barb said she was going to go to her room. "You girls stay up as late as you want," she said. "I know how girls like to stay up and talk. You just get to know each other."

As soon as Aunt Barb was gone, Celia mimicked me: "Yes please! I'd just *love* to watch *Beauty and the Beast.*'"

"I like it," I said. "I really do."

"Oh please," said Celia. "I'm going to go get a real movie from my brother's secret stash."

It wasn't that I was afraid of what she'd come up with exactly, I mean, I'd be interested to see some of that kind of thing someday, but I didn't want to spoil my chances for Celia visiting me and me coming back to swim with Trane and the Robinsons. Also, it seemed like a good idea for me to be the one who called the plays with a kid like Celia.

So I told her, "Look, Celia, I have this thing about finishing movies once I've started them. You know, like a superstition." I was making this up as I went along. "I believe that if you don't finish a movie once you've started it, something bad will happen."

"Like how bad?"

"You have to finish, or else something of yours won't finish."

"You mean like your life? You mean you'll die?"

"I didn't say that. It's just a superstition. You know what I mean, right?"

She couldn't possibly know what I meant, because I didn't, but it got her attention. We watched the entire movie, but she kept looking at me. I thought she was going to turn off the movie just to see what happened, so I stayed alert to stop her if I had to.

When it was over, Celia said, "Do you want to do something really fun?"

"Horror movies?"

"No! I don't watch those anymore. I told you, that's how I got over being phobic like my mom. I'm into real life adventure now. I just have to go make sure my mother's asleep. And don't worry, I never get caught."

She came back looking very cheerful. "She's asleep. I knew she would be. She sleeps with her TV on and her lights and the radio but with earplugs and blinders. Come on. I got the keys out of her purse."

"What keys?"

"You'll see."

Celia went through the kitchen to the door that goes into the garage. Instead of turning on a light, she pushed a button, and the garage door opened. It let in a kind of soft but weird glow of darkness.

I said, "What are we going to do, ride bikes in the dark?"

"We're going to ride cars in the dark," she said. She got into the Mercedes Benz, and the car growled gently as she turned it on. The window on the passenger side slid down. "Get in," said Celia, looking tiny and silly behind the wheel. "I'm a good driver."

"You don't have a license."

"Duh! That doesn't mean you can't drive, and vice versa too! My mother has a license, and she's a terrible driver."

A lot of thoughts went through my mind. One was that I should be saying No to riding in the car with Celia just the same as if she had offered me alcohol and drugs. Another thought was, Forget what you *should* do, getting in a car with a nutcase like Celia is stupid!

On the other hand, I didn't want her to think I was a coward.

On the *other* other hand, something in me wanted to do something wild, especially after all those hours of being nice to her mother and watching Disney. So I got in, but I didn't close the door. I said, "What do you do, go up and down the driveway?"

Celia smiled. It was that same smile she had used when I told her she was perverted. "Close the door," she said very softly. "I'm an extremely careful driver. I don't leave Pinnacle Estates. I don't talk when I drive. I only go where it's safe. I drive very slowly."

Of course I was an idiot and a fool, and I imagined Eutreece's head shaking and her tongue clicking if she saw what I was doing. But I closed the door and put on my seat belt.

Celia moved the lever and the car backed out of the garage gently and slowly, down the driveway. She stopped where the driveway met the street. "I mean it about not talking," she said. "I have to concentrate."

I said, "You'd better put on your seat belt."

To my surprise, she put it on before backing out the rest of the way. She put the car in its forward gear, and slowly, almost as if we were floating, we eased around the dark, smooth, swoopy streets of Pinnacle Estates. We opened windows and the sun roof and let the damp night air flow over our skin. We didn't talk and we didn't play the radio. We just slipped through the darkness in the Mercedes Benz.

It seemed to me that Celia actually was a pretty good driver. We went around the circle two times, then down a hill and around some more houses. One house had lights and cars like a party. She stopped and backed carefully into a driveway, and then we went the other way.

The car was dark and quiet, the night smelled good, and everything was like a dream. Just me and Celia in the big car, circling slowly.

"Do you do this a lot?" I said after we'd been driving for a while.

"Only when my dad's away. I can't do it when he's home, because he's a light sleeper. My brother taught me last summer. It's really easy. Do you want to try it?"

"Not me! Not in your car."

We were starving when we got back, so we ate leftover pizza and surfed around on the TV for a while. Then I took a shower in her green bathroom with all the shower heads while she sat in her bed and listened to music on her headphones. After I got in my bed, I didn't think I was going to be able to sleep. I hadn't slept anywhere except with my family since we moved to Fish House Lane. We hadn't even stayed at Mama Mae's, and Eutreece and I didn't have sleepovers because we live so close together.

I didn't know if Celia was awake or asleep, but I could hear high notes occasionally from her music. I was wide awake, smelling the air conditioned air, thinking about driving cars. I fell asleep finally, and I had a dream that I was driving a car as big as a starship with all my family in it. We had a kitchen and beds and a swinging seat for Parker, everything you could ask. Celia and Aunt Barb were there too, and Daddy was the driver and I was his copilot.

The next morning, Aunt Barb gave us sticky buns from the bakery for breakfast. I said I should go home, and Aunt Barb said, "How about one more swim?" And I couldn't say no to that. Driving back, Celia talked about the Robinson Family Fish Fry, Aunt Barb kept saying, "We'll see, we'll see." But I could tell she was going to let Celia have her way.

Chapter Seven
Making Up With Eutreece

As we drove up Fish House Lane, I saw Eutreece on her porch. She didn't raise her head from her book as we drove by. Aunt Barb and Celia only stayed long enough to make plans for Celia coming to Fish Fry. Mom was glad I was back, because she had to take some stuff to Boutique Afrique and Parker was asleep. She said, "I need you to watch him—Trane's in the house, and Parker's asleep on his quilty and Daddy's asleep in the studio."

Our house seemed hot and sticky and a little dusty to me after just getting out of the Mercedes Benz. As I helped Mom carry the bags to the car, I said, "They have a housekeeper."

"Put the shopping bags in the back seat," said Mom.

"And Celia has her own bathroom."

She said, "I don't care if they have ten bathrooms. Are they happy?"

My mother was wearing an orange African headdress to hide her hair. If you ask me, African clothes make her look even whiter, but of course, she never asks me.

I said, "They have six bathrooms and a swimming pool. A swimming pool would make me very happy."

60

She was in a hurry, and got into the car, but rolled down the window to talk to me. "So you think you want your own bathroom and a swimming pool? So you think having a lot of money makes people happy? Do Richie and Barb seem like happy people to you?"

"I didn't meet Uncle Richie."

"My point exactly!" cried my Mom. "He isn't even at home half the time!" Then she started the car and her voice got all drippy like she was about to cry. "Oh Billie," she said, "I hope you aren't going to turn against your own family values! I hope one little trip into consumerism isn't going to turn your head! I don't have time now, we'll have to finish this discussion later."

"I don't want to have a discussion," I said. "I just wanted to tell you about Celia's house."

She drove away, and I thought about how unfair she is. If you say just one little thing, she decides you've turned against your family! Aunt Barb might be phobic, but at least she wore normal clothes from the mall, not home-made wannabe African robes.

Trane came running out to meet me. "Boy, are you in trouble! Eutreece is never going to speak to you again this side of the grave!"

"Who cares?" I picked up my bag and went up to my room. Trane came with me. I was sick and tired of them all, and I'd only been home ten minutes. "*She's* the one who let Panther loose and caused all the trouble. I just went to visit my cousin."

"Eutreece says don't ever come back to the Surveillance Place, it's hers alone now."

"Oh, is that what she said?"

"That's what she said!"

"Well, I say she can just get over it."

Trane shook his head in amazement at my courage.

61

Now my room looked funny to me. It is the first room that was ever all my own, and Daddy painted it to look like a jungle. When we first moved to Fish House Lane, I used to run from wall to wall like a crazy person saying, "This is mine! This is my own room!" But now I looked at it, and instead of seeing parrots and flowers and a river on the floor, I saw spaces between the floor boards and a crack in the window glass.

And only one bed.

When Celia came to sleep over, I was going to have to say, "Here, Celia, put your stuff behind this cheesy tie-dye curtain. And oh, by the way, you have to sleep in the same bed as me."

"Trane, could you please get out of my room?"

He sat down on my bed.

"I mean it!" I said. "Go downstairs and watch Parker. I have to unpack."

"Parker's asleep," he said.

"Then go watch him sleep! I want some privacy." I pushed him out, and he tried to come back in, so I leaned my back on the door. He pounded on it.

"Billie! Billie! I know you're in there, Billie!"

Idiot. Of course he knew I was in there. I hissed, "You're going to wake Daddy!" That shut him up, and after a little while he went downstairs.

I lay down and wondered: What would Celia think of my bed legs carved to look like faces? They're better than a drawer full of toy razor claws and vampire teeth, I thought, but I wasn't convinced.

And where *was* she going to sleep? I mean, I could give her the bed, but then I'd be sleeping on the floor, and that seemed at least as embarrassing as sleeping two to a bed. The only thing that didn't seem embarrassing was to have twin beds so your guest got her own bed.

When Trane and I lived with Mama Mae, I prayed all the time for my family to get back together. I thought if our broken family could get fixed, then everything would be okay forever. If some girl at school was mean to me, or if Mama Mae was too strict and old-fashioned, I would pray to have my family fixed. Sometimes I pretended that Daddy was standing beside me so that I could tell him my problems, and he would make things right.

After I put my stuff away, I went downstairs and stood outside his room again. I stood there a long time, but this time, he didn't wake up and call me.

In my mind he asked how my sleepover was.

In my mind I answered, *I had a good time.*

And he asked, *Would you want to live there?*

And I answered, *No.*

You see, even in my imagination, I tell him the truth, and even in my imagination, he helps me feel better.

When Parker woke up, he first rolled a little bit from side to side and wrinkled his nose. Then he got still, and suddenly his eyes popped open and he smiled like lights coming on in a dark house. I changed his diaper and told him we were going to go for a walk, and I put him in the backpack carrier. He loves to ride around in cars or on people's backs. He just loves to be part of what's going on. He's lucky, because that's all it takes to make him happy.

We went over to Surveillance Place because I didn't intend to let Eutreece tell me what to do. I was half hoping Eutreece would be there, but the place was empty. Surveillance Place seemed dirty again. The floor was muddy, and the green chair with the bent leg was over on its side. I picked it up and moved the lounge chair into its right place, but I didn't sit down.

Parker and I went out and put Panther on her leash, and the three of us started down Fish House Lane toward Robinsons'. I didn't have a plan except to finish the fight with Eutreece so we could make up and get back to normal. The little kids were playing in the middle of the road: Trane and Martin and Hector Hernandez, and Little Bit Robinson was toddling around too with her funny way of almost falling and then stepping in the direction she almost falls in. They had made a fort out of cardboard boxes. Hector was the enemy, throwing chunks of dirt at the fort.

"Stop throwing stuff!" I yelled. "I've got the baby!"

"Hey Billie," said Trane, "Can we have Panther? We need her to be an attacker."

I said, "Panther, if I leave you here, will you be good?" Panther grinned her big drooly dog grin with her tongue hanging out. I unfastened her. Little Bit came with me and Parker. As we got closer to the house, I looked up on the upstairs porch for Eutreece, but she wasn't there. The only person in sight was the oldest Robinson brother on the downstairs porch. His name is Eustace, but everybody calls him Youey. He was sitting on the steps shining the shoes that go with his security guard uniform. He's the one who is going to go to the Police Academy. His girlfriend is already a police officer, and she's helping him study for the test.

I said, "Hi, Youey."

"Hi, Billie," he said. "Are you all ready for the Fish Fry?"

"Yep. My mom is going to bake bread."

"Listen, Billie, tell your mom she needs someone to look at the exhaust system on that car. I saw her drive by, and she's going to lose her muffler." Youey drives a black

Mustang Classic that he rebuilt himself. "Tell your mother I'll look at it, if she wants me to."

"Thanks, Youey," I said. "I'll tell her. Is Eutreece upstairs?"

"She was on the upstairs porch a minute ago."

I figured she had seen me coming. That was like her, when she was mad at me, to hide if she saw me coming. Little Bit and I went in the house, which smelled delicious. They were already cooking for the Fish Fry. I went straight upstairs past the Robinson graduation pictures and the special blank space next to Youey's high school picture for when he makes police officer.

I looked in Eutreece's room first, but no one was there. She's got shelves of books and stacks of books. Little Bit made a noise and ran down the hall toward the porch. Eutreece was out there. She had sneaked back out onto the porch again! She had her legs up on the railing and was wearing sunglasses and pretending like she'd been there all along.

"Oh," I said. "You're back on the porch."

She looked at me through the sunglasses.

If she said nothing, that would mean she was *really* mad. But luckily, she said something. "Well, well, if it ain't Miz Limousine White Lady."

"Listen, Eutreece, I went to visit my cousin! You don't need to make remarks." Eutreece opened a family size bag of tortilla chips and crunched on a big handful. "I was being nice to my cousin after *somebody* let the dog loose and about scared her to death."

Little Bit went over and got some chips, and Parker started to make some noises like he was hungry too.

"You didn't go to her house to be nice to her," said Eutreece. "You went to her house because you want to be like her."

65

"I just wanted to find out about her!"

"You think you can go be white one day and come back home the next day."

"We watched movies and ate pizza and swam. That's not a color!"

"Ha!" said Eutreece.

Meanwhile, Parker started to whimper because he always wants to do what everyone else is doing, especially if it's food. I said, "Parker would like a chip, please."

She shrugged. I got him a chip, and he started chomping it and making a mess all over my clothes.

I said, "Besides, if I ever did to your cousin what you did to my cousin, you'd *really* never speak to me again."

"What? What did I do to your cousin?"

"You let Panther loose!"

"You think I let loose Panther? You think *I* let loose Panther?"

"Actually, I thought it was hilarious, the way Celia squealed like a mouse. She's an extremely weird girl, Eutreece. And she loves it if you tell her she's perverted."

Eutreece made a tooth-sucking noise.

"She sneaks into her family's car at night and drives it in the dark. But also she's this big coward about leaves that fall off the tree into her pool. Also, she's obsessed by horror movies. She collects vampire teeth and Freddy Kreuger claws and all kinds of junk. And her house, well, you ought to see her private bathroom."

Eutreece loves houses. My mom didn't want to hear it, but Eutreece did. Eutreece is always planning what her mansion is going to have in it someday when she becomes a rich detective or lawyer. I had stuff to entertain her for months: the bushes in shapes, the four shower heads. She should be the one living in Celia's house. Aunt Barb would love her vocabulary and her appetite.

66

I said, "The swimming pool is for the whole family, of course, but her bathroom is just hers. And the pool has its *own* bathroom in a little house that also has a bar. With beer in the refrigerator, and Celia insists she drinks it whenever she feels like it."

"Did you see her drink it?"

"No, but I saw the beer."

Eutreece started asking things like, "Did you say there's a wet bar at the pool or just a refrigerator?" and "Did you say wall-to-wall in her bedroom and game consoles *and* her own computer?"

I said, "Yes, but she's lonely."

Eutreece took her sunglasses off when I said that and just looked at me.

"Really," I said. "She's lonely by herself. She's going to come and visit tomorrow, and I promised she could meet you."

"Tomorrow is the Fish Fry."

"Your father told me I could invite anyone I wanted to, and I did."

Eutreece brought her eyebrows down low and stuffed her mouth with chips and made big crunching noises, but she didn't say she was going to uninvite me. She crunched for a while, and Parker went uhh-uhh for more chips.

Eutreece said, "Someday when I have my mansion, I'm going to have a private race track with miniature sports cars where my children and their friends can drive in perfect safety."

I said, "I don't know if I want to be really rich."

"Everybody wants to be rich. It's logical!"

"Not my mother."

"Oh, your mother!"

I looked at her hard to make sure she wasn't going to insult my mother. I said, "My mother says rich people get

67

bored too easily. I mean, like Celia is always looking for things to do. That's why they came out here to get me. Celia was bored."

Little Bit had wandered off downstairs, and Parker was starting to fuss. "Let's go get lunch," said Eutreece. "We can take it to Surveillance Place and make a plan."

There were boxes of soda stacked beside the kitchen door, and on the stove were pots of barbeque sauce and boiling eggs and potatoes. Aunt Lucy was peeling potatoes.

"Good afternoon, Aunt Lucy," said Eutreece.

"Good afternoon, Aunt Lucy," I said.

"Good afternoon, children," said Aunt Lucy.

What you have to realize about Aunt Lucy is that she is Eutreece's father's *grand*mother's sister. She is the oldest person I ever met, and she knows how to read every long word in the Bible.

Eutreece got out a grocery bag and took some fried chicken from the refrigerator. Aunt Lucy didn't say anything. Eutreece packed a plastic bag of crackers. Aunt Lucy still didn't say anything. But when Eutreece got out a two-liter grape soda, she said, "You children drink too much of that purple stuff! It rots your teeth!"

"The soda's not for me, Aunt Lucy," said Eutreece.

"Don't you lie to me, Little Bit!"

Now, it's Eutreece's baby sister who is called Little Bit, but Aunt Lucy calls anyone whatever she feels like. She is always making up names for people. Eutreece said, "It's not for me, Aunt Lucy, it's for *her*," and she pointed at me!

Aunt Lucy closed one eye and sucked her lips in and out. "Well, it's no good for Shirley Temple either." Her nickname for me is the little movie star from the very beginning of movies, which I guess was when Aunt Lucy was a little girl herself.

Parker started laughing. He really likes Aunt Lucy because she makes faces for him. She pulled her lips back with two fingers. All you could see was gums and one tooth halfway back on the top and one on the bottom. Parker reached for her. "That's right, baby," she said to Parker, squeezing his fat little hand. "You got intelligence! You and me, we don't have many teeth, but we got intelligence! These young people today, they got purple soda pop sloshing round their brains."

Eutreece said, "See you later, Aunt Lucy," and started out the door.

When we were outside, I said, "That was real nice, Eutreece, blaming me for the soda."

"I gave it to you mentally."

"Well I may not let you have any of my soda."

"I may not let you have any of my fried chicken."

A car horn honked when we were halfway to my house. It was my mother coming back. As soon as he saw her, Parker started making his little I-want I-want whimper. He's perfectly happy to go around with me if Mom isn't around, but the minute she shows up, he can't get away from me quick enough!

So Mom took Parker in the car with her, and Eutreece got in too, but I had to catch Panther. As I dragged her down the road, she kept trying to kiss me. By the time I finally got her tied up, I was hot, sweating, and covered with dog spit.

Meanwhile, Eutreece was relaxing on my porch watching my mom nurse Parker. Mom said, "I offered Eutreece some tea, but she doesn't want any."

I said, "We're going to have snacks in the Clubhouse."

We always call it the Clubhouse in front of the adults so they will think it's kid stuff. I was hot and covered with dog spit, but at least the fight with Eutreece was over. I didn't know what she'd think of Celia in person, but that was tomorrow, not today.

Chapter Eight
Neighbor and Hassan

When we got to Surveillance Place, we had to clean it up again before we could eat. Eutreece shook her head. "The little potato heads are coming in here and messing it up. They should be banned." We started off on a discussion about whether or not to ban the little boys. As we discussed, we swept out some of the mud on the floor and propped open the spy window blanket with the broom handles and put our food on the Christmas can like a table. We each got a chicken breast, a thigh, and a leg, plus three wings. I don't know how Aunt Lucy does it, but every bite of her chicken is perfectly crispy on the outside and perfectly juicy inside. We also had some crackers and drank the grape soda.

After I had slowed down on eating, I told Eutreece more about Celia's house, especially about swimming in her pool. Eutreece asked questions about the house. What about the maid's room, what about the separate sub-zero freezer in the kitchen, what appliances they had. She wanted more information than I remembered. I said, "You'll just have to make friends with Celia tomorrow and get invited to swim."

We took a little break from talking, and Eutreece finally finished eating. We wrapped what was left for later and put it in the can. She said, "I think it's time to go check out Neighbor."

"Oh Eutreece, even if he did bury something or hide something, he already dug it up."

"We have to find out what's going on at his house."

I said, "Why? I mean, why do we have to?"

"Why? Because we do Surveillance, that's why, and because something funny is going on."

Even last week I was just as much into being Spy Girls as she was. We read spy books and got Eutreece's brother Youey to drive us to the multiplex downtown to see spy movies, and we drew pictures of spy outfits with a lot of black stretch leather and spike heels. But now, all of a sudden, like somebody turned a switch, it wasn't as interesting to me.

It was probably just the hot weather, I thought.

Or else, something had happened to me during that slow blue swim in Celia's pool. Then I thought: What if my white side was coming out? What was your white side like, anyhow? My hair was the same: wide and wild and the same color as me. My skin was, if anything, darker after being out in the sun all day in a bathing suit. I had always thought that if I had a white side, it would be sort of sappy and singing sad songs like my mother. What if my white side meant I wanted to stop spending time at Surveillance Place and go live in a fancy house and leave my best friend behind? What if my white side was a sickness like Daddy's that you never knew when it was going to mess you up?

That's not you, Billie Lee, I told myself sternly. Eutreece is your best friend, even if she's a little bit stuck on this spying stuff.

So even though I was hot and sticky and didn't care too much about Neighbor and his Bargain Bob bag burial, I said, "Well, let's not just sit around and talk about it, Eutreece. Let's take the boat down to Neighbor's."

So we did. We got in our old row boat and pushed off into the canal, which was looking even browner and yuckier than usual. Eutreece sat at the squared off end and I rowed. When you're rowing, you're backwards, and you have to depend on the other person to tell you where to go. It was buggier than the last time we went down and spied on him. Over on the bank was a dead car and then some dead tires without their car and a lot of roots that were the same brown color as the water.

Eutreece waved her hand to the bank, which meant for me to pull in at the little piece of land that sticks out where you can hide the boat. Neighbor's House is on the same side of the canal as the other houses, but you can't see it from Fish House Lane. He has a little tiny road of his own, but he doesn't have a car. We pulled the boat up on some roots. At least this time I was wearing my old sneakers. We tied the boat to a dead tree root and crept through the weeds to a little path. Pretty soon we could see the tarpaper roof of Neighbor's house and a truck parked next to the house.

We stopped when we heard voices. Mostly it was Neighbor making one of his speeches where his voice goes like a word-waterfall that reverses direction in the middle and starts all over. There was another voice too that interrupted him and sounded angry. We bent down low and went closer to see who it was. They were on Neighbor's porch which sticks out over the canal. Neighbor was wearing his usual ratty old suit jacket and old-fashioned man's dress-up hat that he wears no matter how hot the weather.

The other man was a lot younger, and he was wearing a Jets sweat shirt and a Yankees cap. Chunks of hair stuck out from underneath the cap, and whenever he said anything, he included a few curses. Neighbor wasn't making much sense as usual, but it seemed to be about money and how a person has to be responsible, and money comes to those who have money, and God bless the child that's got its own.

The younger man, who was facing us, seemed to be trying to convince Neighbor of something, cursing a lot, and standing up and sitting down.

And when Neighbor wasn't making a speech, he was saying, No, No, No.

It was really itchy in those weeds. I felt a sneeze coming on, but I didn't sneeze. I did move myself a little bit. I don't think I moved much, and we were probably too close to the house anyhow, but all of a sudden, the younger man stopped talking and looked straight at us.

"Somebody's out there—" he said, and before we could even stand up he had jumped off the porch, right over the railing. I was already running, but Eutreece never runs, and I heard him grab her and curse her, so I had to make myself stop and turn around. He was giving her a shake and saying, "Who are you? What are you doing here?"

My heart was pounding like I'd run a mile instead of ten feet, and Eutreece went very still: that's what she does when she's in trouble.

I ran back and started yelling, "Mr. Neighbor! Mr. Neighbor! It's just us! Mr. Neighbor, it's Eutreece Robinson and Billie Lee!"

Neighbor caught up and said, "Aw, it's just them kids again, Hassan."

74

And suddenly I realized that this was Neighbor's famous son who he always talked about, who was supposed to have had a chance to be a professional baseball player only something had happened. I never remember how the story went at the end or maybe Neighbor hadn't told us that part.

Hassan let loose of Eutreece, but she stayed right where she was, still not moving. It always surprises me when there is someone bigger next to her, because I think of her as big, not like a little kid.

Everybody was frowning. Hassan's face twisted up, and Neighbor's old reddish brown skin has lines almost down to the bone, and his eyes are always hidden in the shade of the hat.

"Okay," said Hassan. "So you know them. Why are they sneaking around the house?"

Eutreece finally moved. She crossed her arms over her chest. "We came to invite Mr. Neighbor to the Robinson Welcome to Summer Fish Fry tomorrow."

Neighbor made a funny snorting noise, and worked his mouth around like he was gearing up for another waterfall speech. "Come up on my porch now," he said. "You all come up on my porch and I'm going to talk to you and him. This here's my son Hassan."

I know I should have just kept my mouth shut, but I said, "Are you the baseball player?"

"No," said Hassan.

"Yes," said Neighbor. "You all children come up on the porch now."

So Neighbor led us and Hassan followed up, and Eutreece and I sat down side by side on a wooden box, and Hassan leaned his butt on the railing of the porch and glowered at us.

And of course Neighbor made a speech.

75

Some of it was his old story about how Hassan could still be a baseball player if he would only get his stuff together and, oh, how he could pitch *and* bat—

"I'm through with all that," said Hassan. "Get used to it."

But Neighbor went on. How great Hassan played in high school and how he got a scholarship to college and how the Yankees farm team wanted him and all he had to do was put out his hand and take the opportunity—but then Neighbor sort of started preaching, and pretty soon he was pointing at me and Eutreece and saying what good children we were and we never gave offense to our parents and how a child who gives offense to his parent is a child of the devil, and I wondered what Celia would think of that kind of talk.

And meanwhile, Hassan just kept shaking his head and saying, "That stuff is all over," only he didn't say Stuff, he said the other word.

Neighbor went on and on, and I was feeling itchy and awful, but Eutreece held still as a stone. Finally, right in the middle of Neighbor's speech, Eutreece stood up and said clear as a bell, "Well, Mr. Neighbor, thank you very much, and don't forget to come to the party."

I was actually feeling sorry for Hassan, because he looked as itchy and twitchy as I was, so I said, "You too, Hassan. Eutreece's dad invited everyone."

We didn't say anything till we were out in the canal, and then Eutreece said, "Now why did you invite that sorry Hassan to my family's Fish Fry?"

"I felt bad for him. Neighbor goes on and on about how he should have done something different."

She snorted. "Neighbor, he's just a old wino, but that Hassan, he's a drug addict, and I don't want to see drug addicts at my family Fish Fry." She said drug addict with

76

her mouth off to one side like she had a mouthful of bugs. "I hate drug addicts. They're a mess!"

"What makes you think he's a drug addict?"

"Did you see him? Wearing that hot sweatshirt in this kind of weather?"

"My daddy wears long sleeves in hot weather."

"That's what I mean," she said. "That Hassan is *sick*."

It was the first time any of my friends especially Eutreece, had actually said that my daddy was sick, and it made me feel funny, like it was more true because she said so. So I ignored that part, and said, "Hassan didn't look like a drug addict to me," I said. "Besides, my mother says their behavior is a cry for help."

"Is that what she says?" said Eutreece, and I was instantly sorry I'd said it. I could see her just thinking how soft my mother is.

"She doesn't say she *likes* them, just that they need help."

"They're a *mess*," said Eutreece. "That's a drug addict for sure, and he could have been a professional baseball player! Now is that a mess or what?"

"We don't know the whole story," I said.

"I have a hypothesis," said Eutreece. "That means an educated guess."

"I know what it means."

"Here's my hypothesis. I think Neighbor hid Hassan's drugs from him and Hassan is trying to get them back. That's what I think. That's what I think he buried, and that's what I think they were fighting about."

"Well," I said, giving a big pull with the oars to get us up to shore and home, "that's one more reason to stay out of Neighbor's business."

Chapter Nine
The Fish Fry

The next morning my eyes opened, and my first thought was *beds*.

It was Fish Fry day, and Celia was coming to sleep over, and I still only had one bed. I looked around my room and saw the flowers and the parrots and the jungle on the wall and the river on the floor, but compared to Celia's room, it seemed totally empty. Celia has CD players and a wall of mirrors and her computer and her game machine and her television and posters and animals and silver party balloons floating up in the ceiling, and I didn't even have a place for her to sleep.

Trane came in carrying Parker. He dumped him on my bed, and I tickled him, and then Trane climbed in too. For a couple of minutes I forgot my problems and pretended I was a little kid too. We have a game where we put a hat on Parker and pretend he's the daddy and Trane is the baby. The hat makes Parker laugh, and that makes Trane and me laugh, and we laugh for a long time. As we laughed, I thought, if Celia doesn't like my room, she can lump it or leave it.

But just the same, she would need a place to sleep.

In the kitchen, Mom was punching down dough, and Daddy was making oatmeal for everyone with nuts, apples, raisins, brown sugar, and cinnamon. After we ate, Daddy went out to sit on the glider, and I did the dishes. Then I went out and sat beside Daddy. The view from the porch is of the turnaround at the end of Fish House Lane plus tall reeds and in the distance, the elevated highways and railroad bridges. They look as far away as mountains.

I said, "You're feeling good today, right, Daddy? You're going to the Fish Fry?"

"I wouldn't miss it, Darling Billie," he said. "I'm going to have a good day."

We sat awhile listening to the glider screech back and forth. He said, "What's on your mind, baby girl?"

It gives me a shiver, how he knows when something is bothering me. I said, "Oh, nothing."

"Umm," said Daddy.

"It's just, I wish Cousin Celia wasn't coming."

"Then tell her not to come. Life's too short to spend with people you don't want to be with."

"Oh, I like Celia. She's weird, but I like her. It's just that, I mean, the problem is, there's no bed!"

"You have a big bed, Darling Billie."

"Oh Daddy! This is modern times! This isn't like Down South or Back in the day and all the people liked to sleep together! Kids either have twin beds or they sleep over at people's houses in sleeping bags."

"I bet Celia has a sleeping bag."

"Celia probably has ten sleeping bags! But *her* room has twin beds that match!" I told him all about Celia's room. He kept his eyes closed and listened.

When I stopped talking, he said, "Well, then, I guess we'll just have to put up the hammock."

I said, "Do you mean a hammock like in people's back yards?"

"That's the kind of hammock I mean," he said.

Daddy rested for a while after breakfast. He was using the snake cane today, and I thought he was breathing a little loud, but he said he felt fine. And he didn't forget about the hammock. It turned out he had bought this special hammock a long time ago and kept it in a suitcase under his bed. He said, "If you have a hammock, you can always have first class accommodations, wherever you go."

The hammock was hand-woven out of super-strong colored string. All we had to do was put a couple of hooks in the wall, and there would be a special bed for me or any friend of mine who might come.

"Hammocks give natural sleep," he said, getting out his tool box. "Also, nothing can climb off the floor and bite you."

Mom came up to my room too, and we decided together about the best place to hang the hammock. We stood in different parts of the room and tried to feel the best place. I got a tingle in the corner where the jungle painting comes together at a tree with spreading branches. It looked right for a hammock too. We all tried that spot and agreed it was best, so Daddy drilled holes with his big hand drill and screwed in enormous hooks.

I got to try the hammock first, and I could have stayed there forever, but Trane came in, and he had to have his turn, and then Mom and Parker. After a while, Mom and Parker went to bake the bread, and Trane left to go play with his friends, and the last people left admiring the hammock were Daddy and me. He sat on my bed with both hands on his snake cane, and I lay in the hammock looking at the tree he had painted for me. I said, "I think maybe I'll sleep here myself."

"I thought you let the guest choose."

"Umm," I said. I was thinking I might tell Celia the hammock could be dangerous since nobody had slept in it yet. But if she still wanted to be the first one to sleep in it, I'd have to let her.

By barbeque time, Celia still hadn't come, so we decided to go on to the party and watch for her car. I wore my new jeans outfit with shorts and a top like a vest. The new sneakers looked just fine, and luckily Mom had been so busy she never noticed I got them dirty and had to wash them. Trane wore his regular old YMCA Day Camp tee shirt, but the rest of my family looked outstanding. Daddy had a flowing maroon shirt, and Mom chose an African robe that was maroon and pink and black. For once, she just fastened her hair back instead of trying to hide it under a turban. Parker had a little maroon cap from the Boutique Afrique that he kept trying to take off and chew. Mom carried him, and Trane carried the bread and rolls, and I carried two folding chairs, and Daddy walked slow but dignified with the snake cane.

There was already a crowd of relatives and friends and cars at the Robinsons'. Youey and some people were setting up wires and speakers for music, and there were tubs of ice with drinks, and the big grill and four small grills already cooking steaks and burgers and barbeque. And not a single fish as far as Trane and I could see.

Eutreece was over on the front steps wearing silver bracelets and silver earrings. Her hair was a work of art with all kinds of loops and waves and braids, but her face looked hang-down.

I went right to her. "What's the matter?"

81

She said, "My mother had to work."

"On Fish Fry day?"

"They couldn't get a substitute, so my mother had to stay with that old woman she works for. That old woman who was supposed to die two weeks ago already. My mother *never* missed Fish Fry before."

I sat down to be sad with her. Eutreece doesn't get sad very often, but when she does, I'm about the only person who can make her feel better. I didn't say anything. I just sat down so I could be there if she needed me.

Just when I thought maybe she was feeling a little better, the silver Mercedes Benz came slowly up Fish House Lane. It was driving in the middle like it was afraid to touch the sides.

I said, "Here comes my cousin Celia."

Eutreece still looked sad, but I had to go greet my guest. Trane and Martin had run out in the middle of the lane and were waving to stop the car, and my Mom was running out too.

Aunt Barbara didn't even pull over, she just sort of stopped in the middle of Fish House Lane. She and Celia got out of the car, but left their doors open like they might get back in at any moment. Everyone was watching them out of the corner of their eyes because they didn't want to be impolite, but you have to admit that Aunt Barb and Celia stood out in the crowd: Celia was wearing black again, except she had a neon green shoulder bag. I ran past Mr. Robinson's giant grill with the ribs on it, past my dad who was sitting in a lounge chair holding Parker. "Celia's here!" I yelled.

Mom was already hugging and kissing and jabbering with Barbara again like they hadn't seen each other only yesterday. At least this time Celia's outfit was a top and pants instead of the long skirt and Halloween hat.

I said hello to Aunt Barb. "Oh Billie!" she said. "Celia isn't sure—"

I grabbed hold of Celia's neon green bag and pulled her towards the party. "Thanks for bringing her, Aunt Barb! Thanks for having me at your house! Good-bye!"

I hadn't been sure I even wanted Celia, but after all the worrying and getting Eutreece mad and putting up the hammock and everything, I wasn't going to let her just drive away.

She kept craning her head from one side to the other while I said "Hi" to different people and "This is my cousin Celia."

Aunt Barb waved and yelled something, but you couldn't hear it over all the talking, so I just waved back.

"Hi, Mr. Robinson," I said as we got to the big grill. "I'm real sorry Mrs. Robinson can't be here. This is my second cousin Celia. You said bring all your relatives, and I did!"

Mr. Robinson showed his gold tooth when he smiled. "Pleased to meet you, young lady. I hope you brought an appetite."

Celia sort of stared at him with her mouth open and then stared at the ribs, not very politely, so I pulled her away from him.

Aunt Lucy was putting a bowl of baked beans on the table. I introduced Celia to her too, and she made little grunting noises and said, "I'm going to call *that one* Little Orphan Annie. You better give Little Orphan Annie a big plate of fatback!"

Celia still hadn't said a word. She seemed small and not worth all the fuss. I don't mean I didn't like her, but she had been bigger in my mind when I was at her house and bigger still when I was worrying about where she would sleep, and now she just seemed sort of small and stupid and I was thinking I was going to have to drag her around all day instead of eating till I bust and relaxing and dancing.

I said, "I got a hammock for tonight, Celia, and I'm going to let you sleep in the hammock unless you like the bed better."

She just stared.

Eutreece wasn't where I had left her. Instead, Arlease the police officer, Youey's girlfriend, was standing where Eutreece had been. "Hi, Arlease," I said. "Have you seen Eutreece? This is my cousin Celia."

Arlease had seen Eutreece go around to the back, so we went that way, me still pulling Celia by her green bag. Out of the corner of my eye I saw the Mercedes Benz making a big slow U-turn and my Mom waving good-bye to Aunt Barb.

Eutreece was sitting on the back steps with a plate of food. She had ribs, chicken, rice, burgers, and a piece of steak so huge it lopped over the edge of the plate. I sort of put Celia in front of Eutreece and caught my breath. They were like opposites in every way except shades. They were both wearing shades.

"Well!" I said. "I finally got you two together! Eutreece, this is my cousin Celia! Celia, this is my best friend Eutreece!"

Eutreece grunted, and Celia said, "She's the one who scared me when I was in the car."

Eutreece sucked barbecue sauce off the fingers on her left hand and said, "Where did this child come from, Billie?"

I could see they were both going to be awful: Eutreece talking to me, not Celia, and Celia staring like no one taught her any manners at all. I tugged on Celia's green bag. "Let's go eat. What do you want to eat? A hamburger?"

"I don't eat meat," said Celia.

Trane and Martin had come around the house in time to hear her say that. Trane said, "How come you don't eat meat?"

"Meat makes me sick to think of. No one should eat meat. Why would anyone want to eat an innocent animal?"

Eutreece started to smile. A little barbecue sauce was making her cheeks shiny. Her smile is just like her father's, but without the gold tooth. First she sucked gently on the end of a rib. "People who don't eat meat lose all their color," she said. She put the rib back on her plate, put the plate down on the step, and picked up her steak with both hands. She bit into it and shook her head from side to side like she was getting a good grip with her teeth. "Mmm that's good," she said. "I *love* meat. I couldn't live without meat! You'll die of bone skinniness, if you never eat meat. *And* lose all your color."

I don't think Celia was getting the part about color. I guess the good thing about them being so different was that Celia didn't even know when Eutreece insulted her.

Celia said, "I'd die before I'd put a dead animal in my mouth."

Eutreece said, "Well, I sure wouldn't want to chew on a live one."

Martin and Trane thought that was just hilarious. They laughed and did high fives and low fives and every which kind of hand slap.

I said, "You only eat like bread and vegetables?"

"I hate vegetables," said Celia.

"So what do you eat?" asked Trane.

"Macaroni and cheese. Pizza."

85

"What about pepperoni?"

"No! That's meat."

"How about pancakes?" I was thinking about breakfast tomorrow morning.

"I like pancakes and French toast and all kinds of desserts."

Eutreece shook her head and spoke to me, as if Celia still hadn't learned English, "How old is this child, Billie? She's so—undersized." I knew that Eutreece meant by that she didn't have even the beginning of breasts yet.

Celia answered for herself. "Older than you could guess."

Eutreece looked her over, from the top of her flat brown hair, down over her bony shoulders and black tank top to her skinny ribs and black cropped pants, white ankles and black sandals. And toe nails painted kind of blacky-red. "I don't know," said Eutreece. "She looks about six to me."

Trane said, "That's younger than me!"

"Naw," said Eutreece, "I mis-guessed. I think she's only about four years old."

"Three!" shouted Trane.

"Two!" said Martin. "One! Zero!"

And then, of course, the potato heads made the sound of an explosion and fell on the ground laughing. Celia straightened her back and crossed her arms over her flat chest. "You can't tell the age of a witch by looking, you know."

She said this in a really hollow way that made the little boys get silent. Martin Robinson even looked a little bit frightened, and Trane said, "You're not no witch, you're my cousin!"

I didn't correct his English.

Celia said, "Oh, I don't expect you to believe me, but—I *am* a witch."

Eutreece made a sucking sound with her teeth. "You know what, Billie?" she said. "You know what? That's the most retarded thing I ever heard. Where did she make that up from?"

Celia pulled the neon green nylon bag close in front of her chest and sort of patted it, like it had something valuable inside. Trane nudged Martin, and they both stared at the bag. Celia stroked it again.

"What's in there?" said Trane.

"What's in where?" said Celia.

"You know, in that green thing."

"That?" said Celia. "Oh nothing. Nothing I'm allowed to tell children about."

"Retarded," said Eutreece. "Totally retarded."

Martin Robinson is small for his age, so he's always proving he's brave. He jumped over and touched the bag and then ran about ten feet away.

"Martin!" I said. "Be polite!"

Trane said, "There's nothing in there. You're my cousin!"

"How do you know there's nothing in there?" said Celia.

I decided I'd had enough of this nonsense. I said, "I'm hungry. Are you hungry, Celia?"

"I want to see what she eats!" said Trane.

"I want to see what's in *there*," said Martin, coming closer again.

But Celia just tucked the bag tight under her arm. We went over to the food tables. Eutreece got a refill. I never saw so much good food in my whole life. There were burgers and hot dogs, *huge* steaks hot off the grill, and big platters of ribs with Mr. Robinson's own secret Down

South sauce. There was country style potato salad (that means it has hard boiled eggs in it) and cornbread and white bread and whole wheat bread (my mother's, which is just as good as white bread). There were baked beans and rice and Aunt Lucy's collard greens cooked up with pork bones and fatback. I don't like greens usually, but I make an exception for Aunt Lucy's collards.

The desserts had their own table! I wouldn't even look at the desserts till later.

I took just a small piece of steak, not to offend Celia. To my relief, Celia didn't seem to have any trouble finding things to eat. She had rolls and cornbread and potato salad. Eutreece pointed at Celia's food. "That child eats food the same color she is," said Eutreece.

I was getting tired of Eutreece making remarks about people's color, but Celia just kept shoveling potato salad onto her plate, and the little boys poked each other and laughed like they were going to choke.

"Mules!" called out Aunt Lucy. "Y'all children sound like a yard full of mules."

"Yes, Ma'am," said Eutreece, and everyone laughed again, and Aunt Lucy laughed, and Daddy and Baby Parker laughed and Little Bit Robinson came toddling over to see what was so funny, and she did her little lurching dance and everyone started laughing again.

Eutreece and Celia and I sat down on a bench under the big tree to eat. People were still coming to the party. Mama Mae came, dressed up with a sun hat and a sun dress that had a little sun jacket. Everybody treated her like she was someone special and got her a chair beside my dad and I took Celia over to say hi to her, and Celia got in good with her by pulling a digital camera out of her bag and taking a picture of Mama Mae and Parker and then of our whole family.

So things improved. Celia and I got seconds and Eutreece got thirds, and we went back to our bench to eat, and once or twice Eutreece even made a mistake and said something directly to Celia.

Finally, we took a break from eating. We were just sitting with our backs to the tree when Eutreece hit me in the arm with her elbow. Coming up Fish House Lane on foot was Neighbor! His old-fashioned winter hat and jacket looked even weirder than usual with everyone else wearing Welcome to Summer clothes.

As he got closer, we could see that he was carrying a plastic Bargain Bob bag.

Neighbor sort of turned away when people spoke to him. He grabbed a roll here and something to drink there, looking around each time like he thought he was stealing although, of course, the food was out there for people to eat.

Celia noticed us noticing. "Who's that?" she said.

"We call him Neighbor," I said. "He has a house down by the canal. He's like a hermit."

"He looks interesting," said Celia. "I collect interesting people, you know. I snap a photo and sometimes interview them a little."

"That's so not polite," said Eutreece. "Don't you have a mother to teach you how to behave, girl?"

"Yeah, I have a mother. She's pretty weird too."

I laughed and Eutreece shook her head. I said, "I wonder if he's got it with him, that thing."

"What thing?" said Celia.

"Nothing," said Eutreece, frowning at me.

Celia said, "Something in that plastic bag?"

I said, "It's nothing."

"What's in it?"

Now Eutreece was really giving me the look. I shouldn't have even mentioned it, but sometimes my mouth just opens and out things come, almost like part of my brain wants to get things moving even if another part of my brain says *Keep still*. So I definitely know I shouldn't have said the next thing, but part of me was still hoping to get Celia in with me and Eutreece. Besides, secrets are always more interesting to tell than to keep.

I said, "Eutreece saw him bury a Bargain Bob bag like that once. But then he dug it up."

I didn't look at Eutreece.

Celia said, "Wow, what do you suppose is in there?"

"Nothing," said Eutreece. "Ab-solutely nothing."

I said, "He's crazy enough that it's probably his teddy bear from when he was a baby."

He was certainly acting crazy, walking around with one shoulder higher than the other, then sort of sneaking alongside the food, and then sneaking a burger off the platter.

Celia said, "Let's go closer and see if we can tell what's in the bag."

"You see?" said Eutreece to me. "You see what you did? Leave it alone, girl."

"It's really nothing, Celia," I said. "It's just a crazy old man. You don't want to scare him."

"Yes I do," said Celia.

But then a pick-up truck came up the road, and stopped at a distance from the cars. And who should get out but Hassan! Hassan leaned against his car door and didn't come any closer.

Something strange happened: we three all looked at Hassan—me and Eutreece and Celia—and then, when we looked back the other direction, Neighbor was gone. Just disappeared as far as I could tell. I mean, he probably saw

Hassan too and sneaked off into the tall swamp weeds, but it really seemed like he had disappeared.

"Oh wow," said Celia. "Did you see that? The hermit is gone! Just whoosh! I knew he was interesting! I bet he's an ancient wizard or a warlock."

Youey and some other people started to go over and say "Hi" to Hassan and invite him to the party, but when he saw them coming, he got back in his truck and turned it around and drove away down Fish House Lane.

We watched for Neighbor to reappear, but he didn't. Eutreece kept looking at me and saying with her eyes, *You are in big trouble!* And I tried to say back with my eyes, *She's my cousin,* but Eutreece just shook her head.

They finally had the music ready to play. It was mostly Mr. Robinson's old classic rhythm and blues: Wilson Pickett and the Supremes and the late great Sam Cooke, but every so often Youey would put on something more up-to-date. Whatever they played, though, it could be as loud as we wanted and not a single person cared because everyone from Fish House Lane and beyond was at the party.

People danced wherever they felt like it, even in the middle of the Lane. The Hernandezes were there, and they danced. Mama Mae danced once with Mr. Robinson, and of course Youey and Arlease and their friends danced. Little kids like Trane and Martin and Little Bit danced too, and even my mother danced, but not Daddy. I thought if Daddy would dance, I'd be totally happy, but he sat with his cane in his left hand and looked quiet and dignified and handsome. I sat with him for a while, but he told me to go dance.

The only other person who didn't dance was Celia, but she took pictures. Some people thought she was a reporter! I stopped worrying about her and went ahead and had fun. Once, when I looked up, Celia was talking to Aunt Lucy. Or maybe collecting her. And once she took a picture of Arlease dancing with Youey and a picture of Eutreece dancing all by herself.

After we had all danced as much as we wanted, we went over to the dessert table where there were all different colors of icing on the cakes plus a row of Aunt Lucy's sweet potato pies. Celia was a little doubtful about the bright orange color, but she tried a piece. She ate her second piece a lot faster. She ate piece number three from her hand without even a plate, and then she took close-up pictures of the pies.

Aunt Lucy said, "That's right, Little Orphan Annie, you build up some flesh."

It was a good party, even with Eutreece not being very polite to Celia and me saying things I shouldn't have said and Celia acting weird enough for someone to collect *her*.

Finally Eutreece's mom came, and they had saved all her favorite Fish Fry foods. Mom and Mama Mae took Parker and Daddy home in Mama Mae's car, and a lot of other people left too, but there were enough still there for Mrs. Robinson to have a good time.

I hope I always live close enough that I can come to the Robinson Family Welcome to Summer Fish Fry—but hold the fish!

Chapter Ten
That Night at Billie's

When it got dark, Eutreece got stuff from her house for the sleepover, and we went to my house. Trane stayed a while longer, and as we walked down the road, we met Mom and Parker and Panther coming back to the party. Panther was all excited to get to go to the party, finally. Mom told us she'd bring Trane home after while, and Mama Mae was sitting with Daddy, and we should be quiet because Daddy was tired.

After we had separated, Celia said, "What's wrong with your dad, anyhow?"

Mostly people say, "How's your dad doing?" but don't ask for details.

"He gets tired sometimes," I said. "He has to rest."

"Yeah," said Celia, "but what does he *have*?"

Eutreece said, "This little witch person asks a lot of questions."

"What?" said Celia. "I'm just asking."

"That's what I mean," said Eutreece.

I don't even know why I had to answer her, except for being a person who would rather talk than keep secrets, so I said, "He used to be fine. When I was little and we lived in New York City he was fine. But then, I don't know, they had fights, him and my mother, and after the fights, they separated, and when he got sick they got back together."

It sounded all wrong; it wasn't because he got sick that they got back together, at least I didn't think so.

"Oh," said Celia, like she'd heard enough. "Do we have to whisper when we get there?"

"We just have to keep our voices down," I said.

We decided to go look at Surveillance Place before we went in the house, so we quietly put everything on the porch, except Celia wouldn't leave her green neon bag behind.

It was strange going through the high grass in the dark. We mostly go in the daytime. We had tried to sleep at Surveillance place once, but the mosquitoes and the moths and all the creepy crawlies chased us into the house. You can't see much anyhow, once it gets dark in those high weeds. Eutreece and I were sort of giggling and stumbling as we walked over the boards to Surveillance Place, but all of a sudden there was a light, and it turned out Celia had a flashlight in her bag. For the first time Eutreece looked at Celia like she had half sense.

We showed Celia the board path, and how we had made the place stand up with the plywood nailed together. We showed her the blanket door on one side and the blanket window on the other side. Eutreece got the good lounge chair of course, and Celia didn't sit down, so I got my regular chair. I pulled up the Christmas popcorn can so we could put our feet up.

Celia was looking out the surveillance window and waving her flashlight beam all over the place. Then she found a spider in the corner and got all *Eee-Eee-Eee* the way she had when I first met her. Then she started asking questions. "What can you see over there? Is the water deep? What's in the can?"

"We keep food in the can," I said.

"So the wild life don't get it," added Eutreece. "Too much wild life out here." She likes mosquitoes even less than I do, and she was slapping at her arms.

"Can I open it?" asked Celia.

I said sure, but Eutreece said it was too many mosquitoes and she was leaving. She headed straight out, and I held up the blanket, waiting for Celia, but she was popping open the can and flashing her flashlight down into it. "There's nothing in there," I said.

"Yes there is," she said. "Can I have it?"

"I don't care." I figured it was left-over rotten chicken. She fumbled around and finally closed up the can, and then we went back to the house.

Eutreece was waiting for us on the porch. Mama Mae came out when she heard us and said she was going to leave. Daddy was asleep and we girls shouldn't make a lot of noise. My mom had already told us that, but Eutreece and I both said, "Yes, Ma'am," and Celia just stared.

Mama Mae was in a good mood. She was friendly to Celia. "I hope we'll get to see those pictures you took."

After Mama Mae was gone, we had a tour of the house. I showed them Daddy's sculptures.

"Cool," said Celia.

Then we went up to my bedroom, very quietly, shushing each other. Celia really liked the jungle on the wall and the bed legs, and Eutreece showed her how the river ran across the floor, too. They both liked the hammock, and Eutreece said we ought to hang it in Surveillance Place. Celia climbed right in. "I want to sleep here tonight."

So that was that. Celia would get the hammock. Eutreece had brought a blanket, a pillow, and a roll of foam rubber. She set up her bed, and then we took turns in the hammock and talked for a while. Eutreece and Celia seemed to be getting used to each other, although both of them still talked mostly to me. I was feeling pretty good. I said, "Just look at us: Celia is white and Eutreece is dark brown, and I'm a happy medium!"

Now if it had just been me and Eutreece, she would have sucked her teeth and shook her head, but Celia said, "That sounds conceited."

"That sounds stupid," said Eutreece.

Celia threw a pillow at me, and the big surprise was that Eutreece threw a pillow too, and they both came over and sat on me! And believe me, having Eutreece sit on you is nothing to sneeze at! We laughed and tussled around, and I started thinking that I really did have everything just the way I wanted.

After we got tired of fooling around, Celia said, "I bet you two don't know what I have in my bag."

"You got everything and its grandma in that bag," said Eutreece.

Celia went down to the end of the bed and started taking things out of the bag. She pulled out some clothes and papers and the camera.

And a Bargain Bob bag.

I said, "Look Eutreece, Celia's got a Bargain Bob bag like Neighbor had. Do you shop at Bargain Bob too, Celia? What's in your bag?"

"I found it," said Celia. "Just now."

Eutreece sat up. "Where did you find it?"

"I found it in the can at Surveillance Place," said Celia. "You said I could have anything in the can."

Eutreece said, "But there wasn't supposed to be any-thing in the can."

"Billie said I could have it."

I said, "I never put anything in that can."

"Me either," said Eutreece. "Let me see that thing."

Celia's mouth pursed up. "It's mine."

"Oh please," I said. "Just open it up, Celia, and we'll all see what's in it."

So she emptied out the Bargain Bob bag, and inside was a ball of silver foil.

"Open it," ordered Eutreece.

Slowly Celia unwrapped the foil. There seemed to be about a million layers, and Celia moved very slowly, completely unwrapping each layer before the next one.

Eutreece grabbed it from her.

"Hey!"

"It was in our Surveillance Place," said Eutreece. "This is important."

So we gathered close around, and Eutreece unwrapped the last pieces of foil.

Inside was some heavy clear plastic, folded. She un-folded it, and it was like a page from a photo album with little sections. And all the slots were empty except for one, and that one had a picture of a man in it, not a photo, but a colored picture on a card.

"What is it?" said Celia. "I can't see!"

"It's a baseball card," said Eutreece. "That's about how crazy Neighbor is, to go around burying and unburying and hiding baseball cards. Shoot. I thought it was going to be drugs."

"It doesn't have to be Neighbor's," I said. "Maybe somebody else put it in there."

"Wait a minute," said Celia. "Let me see that thing. This is not a baseball card. I mean, this is not just any baseball card, this is a Satchel Paige Cleveland Indians card."

"What's a Satchel Paige Cleveland Indians card?" I said.

"It's a very valuable ancient baseball card."

Eutreece made her eyes so narrow you couldn't see them anymore. I could tell she was thinking. "What makes you think it's valuable?"

"Yeah, Celia, what do you know about baseball cards?"

Celia started to smile. "Satchel Paiges are worth thousands of dollars."

"You don't know that."

"Yes I do. My brother doesn't only collect porn, he also collects baseball cards."

Eutreece took it from her and started looking closely. "I've heard of Satchel Paige. He was famous," she said.

Then I thought of something else. "Hey Eutreece, do you remember what Neighbor said about where his son works now?"

Her eyes and my eyes met: Hassan worked in a collectibles shop!

"Who is Neighbor's son?" said Celia. "What about where he works?"

We sort of ignored Celia. I said, "What if Neighbor stole this card? Or, what if Hassan stole this card?"

"Who is Hassan?"

"Shh," said Eutreece, and she closed her eyes so tight that they disappeared in her cheeks.

"What's she doing?" said Celia.

"She's figuring it out," I said. "This is how she concentrates. She's very good at mysteries, although she prefers murder to baseball cards."

"Do we have to be quiet while she concentrates?"

"No."

"So who's Hassan?"

"He's Neighbor's son who was once going to be a baseball player. He's the one who drove up to the party and then drove away."

Eutreece's eyes snapped open. "I got it," she said. "Hassan stole it. Hassan is a drug addict like I said and they would steal anything. Hassan stole it, and then Neighbor stole it from Hassan to keep him from buying drugs, and now Hassan's trying to get it back because a drug addict would even steal from his own father."

Celia said, "Yeah, but it isn't stealing if his father stole it from *him*."

I said, "So why didn't Neighbor just take it back to the collectibles shop? Why would he hide it in Surveillance Place?"

Celia said, "Because even though his son is a thief and a drug addict, he doesn't want him to get arrested?"

Eutreece and my eyes met, and Eutreece's eyes said to me, *Okay, so your cousin isn't as dumb as she looks.*

But then Celia made a childish devil-face. "I say, let's sell it ourselves and take a slow boat to Europe!"

And Eutreece looked at me again and she was like: *I take it back; she is as dumb as she looks.*

I said, "Do you remember when Hassan came looking for Neighbor? And Neighbor ran off? You don't suppose he would hurt him, do you?"

"His own father?" said Celia.

"That would be patricide," said Eutreece. "That's exactly the kind of thing a drug addict would do."

I said, "Eutreece is prejudiced against drug addicts."

"And white people," said Celia.

Eutreece gave Celia the look this time instead of me. "If something's a fact, then it's not a prejudice. I know what I

99

know," she said. "That's why Satchel Paige is famous. He was the greatest player of all time, and the white people wouldn't let him play."

"Not as great as Willie Mays," said Celia.

"Or Babe Ruth," I said, but then I don't know much about baseball.

"Hank Aaron," said Eutreece.

"Derek Jeter," said Celia.

I could see they were about to get into something long, but even though part of my mind was interested to see where they would go with it, if they were going to end up friends or enemies, another part of my mind was feeling worried about Neighbor. I didn't like the idea of Neighbor getting hurt. He was crazy, but he had always been nice to us kids. It gave me a kind of shiver, that a real person might be in danger.

I said, "Let's argue about that later. We have to figure out what to do with the baseball card. I'm going to ask my Daddy."

"Not an adult!" said Celia. "You don't want to bring in an adult!"

I said, "My Daddy is very cool."

Eutreece shook her head. "We need to think about it some more first. And make some plans."

I said, "Well, I have to check on my Daddy anyhow, while you two are arguing. I'm supposed to make sure he's sleeping okay. If he's asleep, I won't wake him, but if he's awake, I'll ask him for, you know, information. Like, What happens if a person finds a stolen good? What's the next step?"

Eutreece said, "Tell him it's just a hypothetical."

Celia said, "What if he guesses something is going on?"

Eutreece said, "She'll tell him it's a game we're playing. The old folks all think Surveillance Place is just a clubhouse."

I went down the stairs and across the big room past the totem pole people with their African robes flowing down to the floor. I stood outside his studio.

I didn't know if he was asleep or awake, so I just listened for a little while. His breathing sounded different. It was sort of fast, and every time he breathed in, he gave a little grunt like it was hurting him.

Right away, I stopped worrying about baseball cards and started worrying about Daddy.

I thought I heard him saying something, so I went in. His eyes were open, and he was sort of staring at the ceiling like he was watching a movie up there. I said, "Daddy?"

He turned his head toward me, but it didn't feel like he was seeing me. I thought, *Daddy, Daddy, Daddy, Oh Daddy, don't be sick again.*

I knelt down beside the bed and picked up his hand. "You're okay, aren't you, Daddy? You were fine today at the party." I pressed my lips on his hand, but he was making this little pant-pant-pant-groan. I said, "What should I do, Daddy? Should I go get Mom? Do you need the doctor?"

The worst part was how he was looking at me without seeing me. That thing about him that makes it so I can answer my own questions—it was totally gone.

Daddy's very sick, was what I thought.

"Daddy," I said. "What should I do?"

"Billie," he said. "Get her."

And it was like that was all he could manage to say, and it meant *Yes, get Mom— Yes, get the doctor. Yes, I need help.*

I jumped to my feet. "I'll get help, Daddy, don't you worry!" and I ran for the phone.

But at the door to the kitchen, I turned around and ran to the bottom of the stairs. "Eutreece! Celia! Come down here right away!"

They came running, and I yelled, "You have to go get my mom, as quick as you can. My Daddy's sick! I have to call the emergency, but you run and get her."

"Where's the car key?" said Celia. "It will be faster if I drive your car."

Eutreece gave her a funny look, and I was in such a panic I thought *Who cares*, let her drive, so I pointed at the hook with the keys, and she and Eutreece ran out the door, and I called the emergency number.

They made me tell my name and my address and my phone number and even my age, and I had to take deep breaths so I wouldn't yell, *Stop asking questions like a fool* and *Save my father!*

When I got off the phone, Eutreece and Celia were gone, and I knew I had to go back to Daddy. I wanted to run after the car to the Robinsons'. I wanted to be the one moving, not the one waiting. But someone had to be with Daddy. So I went back across the living room toward his room.

The sheet had fallen off his shoulders, and it scared me how bony the shoulder near me was, and his eyes were looking stranger and stranger, like aliens had taken over him.

"You'll be better soon, Daddy," I said. "You have to be." And he was still going huh-huh-huh and I said, "You'll be better real soon," and I patted his arm and had this awful feeling he didn't even know I was there.

It seemed like forever, just him and me in the little room. Mostly I stood back against the wall and watched him, and whenever I could get up my courage, I'd pat his arm and tell him he'd be better soon. It seemed like someone should have come back a long time ago. Daddy closed his eyes, and I didn't know if that was good or bad. "Keep breathing, Daddy," I whispered. "You have to keep breathing, even if it hurts, keep breathing."

He went Huh-huh-huh, only it seemed a little softer. That's because he's relaxing after that awful coughing, I told myself. "Keep breathing, Daddy," I said.

Finally I heard some noise at the door, and here came Mom looking like a ghost and Eutreece with baby Parker and behind them Celia and Trane, and Mom pushed past me and lifted Daddy up in her arms, and told me to get some wet towels, and I didn't know what they were for, but I was happy to have something to do and to have Mom home. She took the wet towels and wiped off his face and arms. She kept telling him he was going to be fine.

Then the ambulance came and the people with the stretcher, and they checked over Daddy, and put a mask over his face to help him breathe, and Mom called his regular doctor and Mama Mae, but Mama Mae hadn't got home yet.

I was standing out of the way with Celia and Eutreece when I saw Trane all by himself in the corner, like a kid getting punished in the funny papers. So I went over and said, "Hey Trane," and he turned around really fast with his eyes scrunched closed and hugged me. I sort of lost my balance, he hit against me so hard, so I let myself sink down onto the floor and held him on my lap like he was Baby Parker. Eutreece and Celia came and sat on the floor on either side of me, and meanwhile, the real Parker had fallen asleep and Eutreece put him on his quilty on the couch even though there were red and blue lights flashing in front of the house and all the noise.

Mom said she was going to leave Parker here so she could ride in the ambulance with Daddy. I had to stay, and Eutreece and Celia were supposed to stay with me, and we were supposed to keep calling Mama Mae till she got home because Mom needed Mama Mae to come to the hospital too.

Then the ambulance people came out with a stretcher with Daddy on it, and I looked closely to be sure they didn't make a mistake and cover his face up with the sheet. They rushed him out, and Mom ran out after the stretcher, but then she came back to say there was a special bottle of milk for Parker if he woke up and cried.

Then Trane cried and hugged her, and she hugged me. She felt damp and smelled different, but it seemed like everything smelled different, especially the house, especially when Mom and the ambulance people and the police were all gone.

Youey Robinson and Arlease came over to ask what the Robinsons could do, and we said Nothing, we were fine. We were going to get a call through to Mama Mae and then we'd go to bed. I realized I really was doing okay, especially with Eutreece and Celia to stay with me and my brothers. But I was afraid of was what was happening at the hospital.

So Youey and Arlease left, and Celia knew some special witches brew tea you made out of regular tea bags and cinnamon and nutmeg. It didn't taste much different than Spicy Icy, but it gave us something to do, and something for Eutreece and Celia to argue about.

Finally, Mama Mae answered, and when I told her what happened, she sort of made a sound like half a cry and half a bark! "Oh, Jesus, hold my hand," she said.

I told her she was supposed to go to the hospital, and she wanted to know who was taking care of us kids, and I told her that Robinsons were keeping an eye on us.

And then, once we'd done what we were supposed to do, it got *really* quiet. I asked what happened when Celia drove the car up to Robinsons, and Eutreece said nobody even seemed to notice. Nobody saw them park, and they just left the key in the car and walked up to my Mom and she was so shocked she ran to the car and never even asked how it got down to Robinson's.

"Your no-color cousin's not a bad driver," Eutreece said.

Celia sort of ducked her head like she was embarrassed to be complimented, then she and Trane played board games for a while, and Eutreece sat with me, and finally we all went to bed in my jungle room.

That was the good thing that night: to have so many good friends in my room together. Celia rolled up in the hammock, and Eutreece had her bed on the floor, and I put Parker and Trane both in bed with me and didn't even care if Parker's diaper leaked or if Trane had an accident. We were about to go to sleep and Eutreece thought maybe we should say prayers and Celia didn't believe in that, so I said everyone should say their own prayer inside if they wanted to, and we did.

After awhile I realized everyone was asleep except me, and that's when I really started thinking sad thoughts.

I kept thinking, *What if he dies?* And then, *But he can't!*

I listened to the clock, and I listened to Parker make a little sucking noise in his sleep, and Trane sort of coughed, and I was still awake.

I didn't think I was ever going to sleep.

105

Chapter Eleven
Billie Wrestles with an Angel

But I did go to sleep, and I dreamed about an angel.

My dream started out with Mama Mae praying and then it turned into a Bible story she used to read to us. It is the story where a man has a wrestling match with an angel. In my dream, I was the one wrestling with this person in a long robe like Mom's African robes, only this robe was all white, and it glowed.

We wrestled and wrestled, and, all of a sudden, the angel jumped away from me and turned into Daddy. He was still wearing the white angel robe, and he laughed and waved and started sort of running away from me and looking back over his shoulder.

"Bye now, Billie," he said. "I have to be going."

"Where are you going?" I asked, and I started to run after him.

He waved some more: "Bye bye, Billie!"

He seemed very cheerful, but he was getting smaller, like someone fading into the distance.

In my dream I yelled, "Don't go, Daddy! Don't go!"

"Got to go," he said, and he started to lose his color and his face and all of him was looking more and more the same color as the angel robe and getting smaller all the time.

I ran my very fastest and jumped like I was going up for a rebound, and I grabbed him around the waist: "Don't you go!" I said. "I won't let you go!"

He kept laughing, and he tried to get loose, but I was stronger. He said very softly, "Now Billie," but I held on as tight as I could.

The tighter I held, the closer his laugh was, and he seemed to get stronger too. Then he said, "Okay, Billie, that's enough now, stop that now, I'll stay awhile." And when he said that, his voice was like a real voice, and I woke up as if he had been standing there beside the bed speaking to me.

I woke up feeling like I'd won the wrestling match.

Chapter Twelve
What Happened

When I woke up it was getting light, and I couldn't go back to sleep. The house felt strange and empty, and we had all slept in our clothes. There was Parker asleep and Trane asleep, and Eutreece in a big lump with her head covered up, and Celia with her thumb in her mouth like a little baby.

I went over to the window, and it was all gray and misty outside. I was looking toward the canal just where our path goes into the weeds.

A man was standing there.

For a second, I thought it was my dream angel, but this was an old bald headed raggedy man, and all of a sudden I realized it was Neighbor without his hat.

I never knew he was bald.

He was just standing there in the fog, staring at our house like he'd been there all night. I stared back at him for a little while, and then realized he could see me too.

He waved. It was a funny wave like, *Come down here, okay?*

I looked back at the others, but they were still asleep. I waved back at Neighbor, and started to go downstairs, but first I went over to Celia's bag and took out the baseball card wrapped in foil and stuck it in my pajama pocket. I wasn't exactly planning to give it back to Neighbor, but it was like I was still in my dream and sort of watching myself do things.

Neighbor was waiting on the porch. I stayed behind the locked screen.

I said, "My daddy got sick last night and had to go to the hospital."

He had the deepest wrinkles around his mouth and eyes I had ever seen, much deeper than Aunt Lucy's wrinkles. I thought he was going to make one of his crazy speeches, but instead, he said in a crackled voice like he was out of practice, "I saw the ambulance. How's he doing?"

I never heard Neighbor say anything so normal before.

I said, "He's going to be okay," even though I didn't really know.

Neighbor sort of looked at his feet and then took a step forward. I jumped back, ready to slam the door.

"Listen," he said. "I need to know. Did you find it?"

Now if it had been Eutreece there, she would have said, just as cool as anything: *Found what, Mr. Neighbor?*

On the other hand, Eutreece would never have gone down to talk to him. Or, if she went, she would never have put the baseball card in her pocket.

I said, "Did you put something in our clubhouse, Mr. Neighbor?"

"I needed a place to keep it safe. And now it's gone." He held his hands out like he was expecting me to put something in them. His hands were a color like red clay. They didn't look very old, but they were very dirty. There was dirt in the wrinkles and dirt in a little line under each fingernail. His hands curled like they needed something to hold.

I said, "What did you put in our clubhouse, Mr. Neighbor?"

He said, "My boy's future."

"A baseball card?" Of course Eutreece would never in a million years have said that, but it was like I didn't care. I didn't want to play games anymore, at least not while Daddy was sick. "Who does that baseball card belong to?"

"It's mine," he said. And then he made one of his speeches: "Once a long time ago, I had aspirations. I owned that store where Hassan works now. I owned it and the one that owns it now worked for me! I had a store," he said, and his hands started to lift up and move around in the air. "It was a good store back then, people came from all over. That man who has it now, he turned it into a pawn shop! A place to sell your jewelry and old radios and TV's! A pawn shop junk store! And I used to have all the great baseball cards! I had a Shoeless Joe Jackson of the Chicago White Sox and once I almost had a Willie Mays rookie card. But my Satchel Paige, that was my best card. I always kept that one card for when Hassan needed to go to college or start a business. That card is Hassan's inheritance."

"So how come he doesn't have it?"

He didn't answer my question, he kept on with his story. "That one that worked for me sneaked up and got my shop and turned it into a pawn shop."

"He stole your store?"

"Naw, I wasn't no businessman. I loved my cards and my banners and my baseball, but I was no good at business. So I lost my store, and that one, he got rich. And

110

Hassan works for him. And all I got left is my one card for my boy's inheritance."

Neighbor's hands sort of stopped where they were drawing pictures, up in the air. He put them in his pocket and his big forehead I'd never seen before got all wrinkled up. "Do you children have my card?"

In my mind there was Eutreece on one side of me saying, *Don't say nothing, you already said too much,* and I knew she was right, I always say too much.

But on the other side was Daddy, and he said, *Give the old man what's his, Billie.*

Neighbor seemed to relax. "You have it, don't you? You children have it? I should of sold it long ago and put the money in a bank. But it's my best card I ever owned. It's a Leroy Satchel Paige. They never made a card for him till after he was past his prime. All the white boys got their cards when they were young men, but Satchel Paige never got one till he was a old man and moved over into the white boy league. That card wasn't the most money card I ever had, but I loved it best."

I unlocked the screen door and stepped outside. It was damp and gray, and I chose Daddy. Eutreece would just have to understand. I think I meant to give it to Neighbor all along or I never would have brought it down. I took the foil out of my pocket and handed it to him. I don't know if I should have. I don't know who was going to end up with it, the bank or Hassan, or if we'd find it back in Surveillance Place next week. But right then, that card belonged with Neighbor.

He grabbed it with both hands and unwrapped it and looked at it up close and far away and then wrapped it up again. "Thank you, young lady. You kept it in A-1 condition."

111

I said, "You could put it in a safety box. My Daddy has some silver dollars his grandfather gave him and he keeps them in a safety box at the bank."

He folded the foil back over the card and looked at the ball of silver foil in his hand and sighed. "That would be a good place for it, I guess. In a bank. Only I like to look at it from time to time."

"Well," I said, "please don't put it in our clubhouse anymore, okay?"

Just then we heard a car engine coming up Fish House Lane.

Neighbor put the card deep inside his coat somewhere, like in a secret pocket. He sort of jumped off the porch to the side and ran off toward the canal. He turned back just for a second and waved, like Daddy in the dream.

"Good bye!" I called after him, because in spite of how much I wanted to know what had happened at the hospital, part of me would rather have stayed right there talking to Neighbor on the porch.

Mama Mae was driving, and my mother was in the passenger seat. In the dim morning they looked like they were the same gray color, and so sad I didn't believe my dream any longer, and I ran out to meet the car.

"What?" I said as the car stopped. "What?"

My Mom got out and came running around and hugging me.

"What?" I said.

"He's okay, Billie," she said, "he's going to make it."

And even though I was hearing the happy words and feeling her around me, it didn't feel happy because Mama Mae was sitting behind the wheel of her car and crying.

"Then why is she crying?"

"Oh, Mae," said my mother, "don't cry, come out here and let's all hug."

And Mama Mae got out of the car, and we all three hugged, skinny strong Mama Mae, soft big Mom, and me.

"He's my baby," whispered Mama Mae. "He's my baby and I didn't do a thing for him."

"Yes you did, Mae," said my Mom.

"But he's all right, isn't he, Mom? He's going to be just fine?"

"He made it," said my mother, and for once, she was the one who seemed in charge instead of Mama Mae. "I want to go back to the hospital to be there when he wakes up. I have to feed Parker, and then I'm going back to the hospital in our car. You saved him, Billie. It was very close."

"Shh," said Mama Mae.

"I knew it was close," I said. "I'm old enough, Mama Mae," I said. "And I already knew it was close and I already knew he was okay."

We all went inside and Mama Mae made a big pot of coffee while my Mom went up to get Parker. Parker nursed like a gobbling pig and Mama Mae started making breakfast. I told them about my dream, and Mama Mae thought it was a religious vision.

Then Mom woke up Trane so she could give him a big hug and kiss and tell him what happened, and Eutreece and Celia got up too. Celia looked like she never got up this early, but everyone wanted to hear the whole story of how Daddy got stabilized, and how, when he came to himself, he asked after each one of his children: Billie, Trane, and Parker.

"He called you his best works of art," said my mom, and Mama Mae got tearful again, but pretended she didn't. Mom had some coffee and toast and left to go back to the hospital, and Parker cried, and we promised him she'd be back soon. Mama Mae kept cooking, and Celia liked the grits and of course the biscuits. It was like Mama Mae was opening a restaurant, she was cooking so much.

The only bad thing was after Mom left and Mama Mae went upstairs to dress Parker, I had to tell Eutreece and Celia about giving the card back to Neighbor. They both agreed that I had spoiled a good mystery and they were sure Hassan was going to get the money in the end and use it for no good.

I said, "It just didn't seem right to me, when you want your Daddy to come back, not to return to people what's theirs."

That made them quiet because they felt bad for me and Trane.

"Well," said Eutreece, "we'll just have to keep a watch on Neighbor and make sure he doesn't do something foolish with his baseball card."

"I thought you were all going to come to my house today and swim," said Celia.

I said, "Trane and I have to go visit my father in the hospital."

"How about tomorrow?" said Celia.

And everyone looked at me, and I said, "If Daddy is better, I don't see why not."

And Trane, the little dope, hugged me because of how much he wants to go swimming in his cousin's pool.

About the Author

Born and raised in West Virginia, Meredith Sue Willis has published many books for kids, including *The Secret Super Powers of Marco* and *Marco's Monster* (both available through Montemayor Press) and *Blazing Pencils*, (a book about writing for students) as well as many books for adults. She teaches writing as a visiting author in many schools throughout the New York City area. She lives in the New York City metropolitan area.

Visit the author's website at:

www.MeredithSueWillis.com/kids.html

Visit Montemayor Press at:

www.Montemayor.com

Printed in the United States
39460LVS00002B/295-345